It Could Happen To You

A Story of Forgiveness and Judgement

Working Through Life Series

Book #1

By Laurie Moede

I dedicate this book to

Nana's 3Cs

that they might understand.

There are several I would like to thank for helping me, inspiring me and loving me through this process of writing.

First and foremost, thank you Heavenly Father for being by my side through everything, every day.

Thank you Holy Spirit for the inspiration You gave me.

Thank you Leah, **Leah Yetter Photography**,

for the cover photo.

Thank you Thea and Chris Adamo, and Debbie Dinges for your input, guidance and editing.

And last, but definitely not least, to my loving husband. Donnie thank you for believing in me. Your support and encouragement means the world to me.

Table of Contents

CHAPTER ONE

<u>MEET THE TURNBAUGH FAMILY</u>

"Cooked vegetables! Ugggg! I really hate cooked vegetables!" Jill protests. *'How can Mom think something that tastes this awful could be good for me? Toni's Mom doesn't make her eat crap like this.'* Jill, being a somewhat determined 11 year old, is certain she knows better than her mother on…well most everything.

Olivia, Jill's 16 year old sister tried to convince her little sister and prodigy in all things for beauty sake, that good nutrition keeps your skin clear and healthy. Yet Jill's still having a hard time choking down the prepared veggies.

Across the table are Levi and Bobby, Jill's 18 and 13 year old brothers. She wishes at times she could have their ability to scarf down anything put in front of them. As she watches them inhale their food, Bobby looks up for an instant and shows Jill his half chewed mouthful of food. With an "Ah-hem" of disapproval from their Mother, Bobby gives her a melt-her-heart grin and continues to clean his plate.

Hanging on every word that Olivia says about eating vegetables to keep your skin pretty, Jill tries another bite. After all, Olivia is very pretty and has beautiful skin. While a lot of the kids her age have acne, Olivia's skin is flawless. So Jill figures Olivia knows what she's talking about, as usual. Olivia isn't just another pretty face though. She's very smart as well. Always on the Honor Roll, a cheerleader, one of the most popular girls in High School. Olivia takes her role as big sister very seriously. She mentors Jill on what to wear, how to fix her hair and what's popular and what's not.

Jill herself is a very pretty girl. At the young age of 11 she hasn't gotten to the age of break outs or changing hormones, but from watching her older sister mature into a beautiful young woman, Jill is confident she will be the same. Jill likes it when people say how pretty she is. She gets a little jealous though when people go on about how beautiful her sister is. This is one reason Jill likes to have her best friend, Toni, around. Toni's not ugly by any means, but she's of the plainer type of pretty. Even the boys at school like to flirt with Jill more than they do Toni.

Jill remembers she has some homework to finish up, so she asks to be excused from the table. Even though the now cold veggies are still on her plate, Mother excuses her. Jill jumps up from the table, gives her Mother a kiss on the cheek and heads off to the stairs. That's when she hears her Father mumble, "I must be chopped liver." This is his way of provoking some attention from his little girl. Jill spins around, throws her arms around her Father's neck and gives him a big kiss on the cheek. Jill teases her Father by saying "You're not chopped liver Daddy! And you're not cooked veggies either! You're more like a dish of ice cream!" This of course makes her Father beam with love and pride. "All right you little smooth talker you! Go get your homework done!" father teases back. With that, Jill's off up the stairs to her room.

Jill didn't really have any homework to do. She just needed to finish up a book that her teacher recommended they try to read by the end of the month. Being the over achieving, straight A student that Jill is, she only has a few more pages to read and it's only the second week of the month. Jill likes school. Getting good grades comes easily for her but the best part about school is the socialization. Being around all her friends, showing her newest fashion accessory, and talking to boys is her favorite part of school. Her parents told her she couldn't date until she was 13 but she already has a secret boyfriend. David Jacobs and Jill don't go out on dates or anything, but they talk in school a great deal and pass notes to each other during class. Everyone knows they like each other, so there's the air of being "in a relationship" that makes her feel more grown up than most of the other girls her age. Now that her brother Bobby isn't in the same school as Jill, it's easier to keep things like having a boyfriend a secret from her family.

Bobby and Jill are closer than most siblings. They hang out together, go places together and actually talk about things more like best friends rather than siblings. It was hard at first for both of them when Bobby went to Jr. High, but they adjusted and found themselves still doing the same things and going places together just like before.

Bobby's a typical 13 year old for the most part. He likes to play rough sports, go fishing and hang out with his friends, especially his best friend, Russel Owens. Russel's sister Toni, happens to be Jill's best friend too. The four of them have known each other since they were toddlers in day care. Dubbed the "Fab Four" they're usually together at any given time.

Bobby and his older sister aren't as close though. Olivia, being the socialite is pretty much the opposite of Bobby. Even though Bobby has plenty of friends, he isn't what people would call a socialite! He teases Olivia on a regular basis about her emphasis on proper social protocols, the latest fashions and excessive amount of time she spends fussing about her looks. Poor Jill is caught in the middle of her older sibling's bouts of harassments. She wants to follow what Olivia says but likes to have the type of fun she has when she's with Bobby.

Then there's Levi. Being the oldest of the Turnbaugh siblings, Levi is expected to lead his younger siblings by example. For the most part he's a good big brother. But Levi struggles with authority figures. When confronted with a problem, Levi tends to lose his temper. It doesn't help that several of his friends have the same attitude. To compound the problem, when Levi gets into trouble, his parents get him out of it.

Levi is a fair student, who keeps his grades up at the insistence of his parents. While he tolerates school, he absolutely loves baseball. Due to an injury his sophomore year though, he had to put up his ball and bat.

Then he discovered coaching. There was an opening for a coaching position for a Little League team the following year, so Levi accepted it. It's strictly volunteer, but Levi doesn't care. He loves the game and now loves coaching almost as much as he loved playing!

Taking this coaching position made Levi's parents very happy. They were concerned, after his injury, he would have too much time on his hands. Since they never expected their children to get a summer job, or a job at any time of the year, he wouldn't have anything to occupy his free time.

Mrs. Turnbaugh, Fran, is a realtor with her own agency. She tried to get Levi interested in real estate. The attempt failed miserably. Fran loves real estate and worked very hard to build her business. She always felt a little guilty for having her young children at daycare so much while she was building her business. But she felt it was necessary. Since the business is doing well now, she can splurge on her children. This makes her feel it was all worth it.

Not that money is a problem for the Turnbaugh family. Nash Turnbaugh started out, at a young age, in the ethanol business. Even while finishing his engineering degree, Nash started working at an ethanol plant in the town where he attended college. Several years later, an ethanol plant was built in the town of Morely, Indiana. Nash was able to get in on the ground floor. To say the least, the money was good, the benefits were great and he's now known as a "big wig" at the plant.

Nash loves his job at the plant but his true love is his children. He tends to spoil them with gifts, a privileged life style and doting on their every whim. He and Fran bought a beautiful house on the edge of town. They loved the wooded acreage in the back. The kids love the pond nestled in the woods where they can swim, fish, and have canoe races in the summer and skating in the winter.

Therefore do not be anxious, saying, 'What shall we eat?' or 'What shall we drink?' or 'What shall we wear?' For the pagans run after all these things, and your heavenly Father knows that you need them. But seek first His kingdom and His righteousness, and all these things will be given to you as well.

Matthew 6:31-33 TPT

CHAPTER TWO

MEET THE OWEN FAMILY

"There it goes!" Toni yelled to her brother, Russel.

"Whoa! There's another one!" Russel ducked as a second bat swooped past his head.

Catching bats had been a common occurrence at the Owens residence since the old house across the street had been torn down. The kids had gotten pretty good at catching bats. But this time was different. There were two bats! The added excitement of two swooping creatures made the task a bit trickier. Good thing they had the added help of Bobby Turnbough who happened to be at the Owen's house. Russel grabbed a fishing net, while Bobby grabbed a badminton racket. Both were jumping, running and swinging their weapons franticly through the air as the nimble flyers dodged their attempts. As the bats flew by the work table, both boys descended on the table. Hitting everything, everything but the bats that is. Objects were launched in every direction. By this time, Toni knew she needed to just stay out of their way. She watched as more items were being rocketed across the room. A can of nuts and bolts scattered across the floor when it was hit like a softball on a batting tee. Then one after another the boys captured the nimble flyers.

"Finally!" Bobby yelled! "I've got one!"

"I've got one too!" In victory, Russel hollered back.

After disposing of the captives, the three kids stood examining the now chaotic condition of the garage.

"Wow! We really made a mess."

"We'd better get busy and clean this up. Mom might be happy we captured the bats, but she'll have a cow if she sees the garage like this." Russel informed the other two.

"Well she's gonna be home in about a half hour. We'd better get busy." Toni told the boys. Toni thought, *'I almost wish I was at gymnastics with Jill right now.'*

That thought is completely out of character for Toni Owen to even think. Toni is, by no means, interested in gymnastics or most any of the other "girly" things Jill is interested in. Jill was able to talk Toni into joining dance class only because she likes to dance. Otherwise, Toni is a "Tom-boy" by nature and makes no apologies for it! She's perfectly happy in her jeans, t-shirt, and her hair in a ponytail. Oh she enjoys an occasional dress up afternoon with Jill and Olivia Turnbaugh. She's even been known to put a hair clip in every now and then. That's about as far as her interests go when it comes to dressing up, fixing her hair and make-up. Especially, make-up! She just can't understand why someone would pay good money for stuff you have to take time to put on and be careful not to smudge. Then wash it all off at night and then do it all over again in the morning. But since she likes being at the Turnbaughs and she really likes being around Olivia, who's the closest thing Toni has to a big sister, she puts up with their nonsense.

As chaotic as the Turnbaugh's home can be at times, what with four kids, Toni enjoys being there. Since Russel and Toni spent a great deal of time at the Turnbaugh's, it's really like there are six kids living there. Sometimes it's better than being at home. Life at the Owen house could be tense at times. There just seems to be something about being at the Turnbaugh's home that seemed more like...well, home.

Jan Owen is a good Mom. She loves her children, Russel and Toni, dearly. With her husband gone most of the time, she has to be both Mom and Dad to them, and that's not always easy. Jan's a quiet, private kind of woman. She works hard at one of the local grocery stores in town. She's able to pick up extra shifts a few times a month, which helps to make ends meet. Jan keeps a clean and tidy home. She really appreciates it when the kids help out around the house. They also take care of the lawn and even though Jan loves to work in her beloved garden, the kids pitch in there as well. It's not a fancy life, but they make do.

John Owen, Toni's Dad, is on the road quite a bit for his job. When he's home, he seems to be angry a lot, complaining about his job, his boss and not having enough money. Russel and Toni tend to steer clear of him when he's in that type of mood. This leaves Jan to put up with his bad temper and his "chip on the shoulder" attitude. There's no doubt John loves his children though. It's just hard for him to show it at times.

The Owens live in the same modest, 3 bedroom house they've rented since Russel was a baby. They like the neighborhood. The yard has room for Jan's large garden and there's a swing set in the back yard. Although Russel and Toni feel they're a bit too old for it now, Toni can be found sitting on the swing with Ruby, the cat, on her lap. Russel won't sit on the swing set any longer, but he'll sit on the ground while talking to his sister. The two of them are very close. Russel watches out for her as much as he can. He may be a bit of a shy young man around others but he's got a wicked sense of humor. He takes great delight in making his sister and Mom laugh. Toni often wishes other people could witness how funny her brother really is.

Russel Owen and Bobby Turnbaugh may come from very different backgrounds and life styles but they're best friends. They compete with each other in sports, but they *always* have each other's back. The Owens and the Turnbaughs support their kids at their sporting events. They sit by each other, cheer their kids on together and are good sports when it comes to winning and losing, but they don't socialize anywhere else. Their paths just rarely seem to cross except for their kids' sports.

They all live in the town of Morely, Indiana. Morely is by no means considered a big town, but it's not a little town either. With a population of 4500, it's flanked by two larger towns just an hour's drive either way. This is where a majority of people go for shopping, entertainment and finer dining. Morely supports 2 grocery stores, 2 discount stores and 8 churches. The Ethanol Plant, where Nash Turnbaugh works, is a major employer of the town. There's 1 High School, 1 Jr. High, and 2 elementary schools.

Like all small towns, everybody knows everybody. And just like high school, there's certain cliques. A handful of families make up the "upper crust", the majority of the families are middle class and then there's the lower class families. The lower class isn't considered poverty level, they just don't have as much as others and don't make as much money as the other families.

The Turnbaughs are in the upper crust category. For the most part they're not rude or terribly boastful about it but they do play the part well. Like everyone, they have "skeletons in their closets", yet they have the means and the social status that allow them to cover up these wrong doings. Remember, everybody knows everybody...and everything. People just play along with the cover up of these indiscretions.

The Owens family are somewhere between the middle class and the lower class. They don't have much in the way of property or fine things, and they're just one major problem away from losing the nice things they *do* have. These are the people who make up the majority of the town and are the ones doing the majority of the work also.

"I have told you these things, so that in me you may have peace. In this world you will have trouble. But take heart! I have overcome the world."

John 16:33 NIV

CHAPTER THREE

<u>IF IT WEREN'T FOR THAT SKUNK</u>

"Jill, we've got to show up the boys this time. I'm tired of them catching more fish than us!" Toni whispers to Jill as the Fab Four head to the pond.

"I agree" Jill replied. "In fact, I think we should try the other side of the pond."

With a look of surprise and disgust Toni responds with, "But it's so swampy over there. It kind of stinks too!"

"I know but Levi told me he had really good luck over there the other day. Plus, Bobby doesn't know about that so he'll think we're nuts for going over there. That way they won't follow us."

"Alright then! Let's give it a try. I'm glad I wore these old sneakers. I'll probably have to throw them away after slopping around in the muck!"

Both girls giggled and hustled to catch up with the boys.

With an air of confidence Bobby asked, "So is there a wager today for most fish caught?"

Matching her brother's confidence Jill responded with, "Sure! What's the wager?"

"Loser has to clean all the fish we catch." Russel chimed in.

"It's a deal!" both girls said in unison, then broke out in laughter.

The boys looked at each other with suspicion. The girls sure seemed confident and took the wager pretty fast. Already they thought something was up. Arriving at the pond, each one prepared their poles as usual.

As they finished preparing their poles, Jill said, "Hey Toni, let's go to the other side and see what we can catch over there."

"Umm" Toni played along, "That's not a bad idea. Let's go."

The boys looked at the girls with surprise.

"You know how swampy it is over there. You're going to sink into the muck and lose your shoes!" Bobby said with a typical big brother tone.

"Yeah, and it stinks over there too!" Russel added and then screwed up his face.

"I'm sure we'll be just fine. We're not that girly that we can't handle a little muck and smell." Jill sarcastically replied.

"Well, *I'm* not that girly anyways. We'll see about her!" Toni joked and nodded her head in Jill's direction.

The boys just laughed and together yelled "GOOD LUCK!" Jill and Toni gathered up their poles and tackle boxes and headed off to the other side of the pond. The kids have been fishing this pond by themselves for a couple years now but they usually stay on the nicer side of the pond. It was known to be a bit marshy where they were going. Mostly after a long rainy spell. But it hadn't rained in this area for a couple of weeks.

The ground was slightly soft, but not as bad as they thought it would be. The smell wasn't as bad either since most of the algae had dried up along with the dirt. A fallen tree lay in the water just a few feet from the shore. They could tell there was a drop off just on the other side of the tree. The girls settled in and began to cast their lines in the water.

"This isn't so bad over here." Jill said with a bit of surprise in her voice.

"Yeah. Last time I was over here my feet sunk so far into the mud, my shoe came off when I pulled them out!" Toni replied as she cast out by the fallen tree.

"Oh! I got a bite!" Toni almost yelled. She didn't want the boys to hear her. As she tried to set the hook she knew the fish was gone. "Rats! It got away."

As she reeled her line in, she saw that the bait was gone. "Well, I'm pretty sure it was a fish and not just a snag. My baits gone."

"I wonder if they're hanging around that log in the water. I'm going to the other side of it and try my luck there." Jill picked up her tackle box and moved down the shore a ways.

"Good idea! Divide and conquer!" Toni said as she finished baiting her hook again.

Within a few casts of their lines the girls had a fish on each line. As they reeled them in they looked over to the other side of the pond. They were pretty certain the boys hadn't caught anything. They hadn't heard them hollering across the pond to boast anyways.

"Woohoo!" Toni yelled "We got the first of many!"

Bobby and Russel looked up to see their sisters each pulling in a fish. Nothing's worse than having their sister out fish them. Even worse was to have both sisters out fish them on the same day. Just then Russel got a bite on his line! He set the hook and started reeling it in. The fish was putting up a good fight. Bobby grabbed the net and helped him bring in the fish. It was a big one too!

"Whoa! Look at the size of this one! It must be the daddy to those little ones you girls are catching! Bobby jabbed at the girls.

It was on! The Fab Four had become the Battle of the Sexes! Both sides of the pond knew they just had to outdo the other. After a few more catches and a couple more hours, Bobby's cell phone rang. It was his Mother telling them it was getting late so they better head home. With several "Awww! It's just getting fun!" The kids gathered up their tackle boxes, poles and fish. As much as the boys hated the fact that the girls did pretty well they were curious to see what it was like on the other side of the pond. They gathered their belongings and quickly made it over to where their sisters were.

Just as they were counting their fish, Jill looked up to see a skunk walking towards them. "SKUNK!" Jill screamed out! The others looked up and saw not just one, but 3 skunks waddling towards them. The four grabbed their belongings, turned and ran! The skunk's waddle turned into a run as the kids were getting away.

"Oh my gosh! Their chasing us!" Russel yelled

The ground was dry enough to walk on but the kids were finding it hard to run on the soft ground. On the other hand, the skunks didn't have any trouble running on it so they seemed to be gaining on them.

"Quick! Climb up this tree!" Bobby hollered at the others. They dropped their gear and the day's catch at the bottom of the large oak tree. The boys gave their sisters a boost up to the low hanging branches, then shimmied up the massive tree themselves.

As they watched the intruders munch on their prized catches, they realized the skunks only wanted their fish.

"We should have just thrown the fish at them." Toni declared

"Then they wouldn't have made us run." Jill added.

After the varmints had eaten a few of the fish, they drug the remainder off into the woods. The four sat still as to not upset the fish thieves and make them give off their nasty perfume. Bobby started examining the tree. It was a massive old oak. The lower branches were sturdy and thick. The trunk was about three feet in diameter and the first branches were about 5 feet from the ground.

"Why haven't we noticed this tree before? You'd think it'd be kinda hard to miss." Bobby asked the others.

"I guess cuz we don't come over to this side of the pond." Jill replied.

"Plus it's kinda back in the woods a little more." Russel added.

"It'd be a great one for a tree fort!" Toni said with a gleam in her eyes!

"That *would* be cool!" Now Bobby had the same gleam in *his* eyes!

"We should ask Daddy if we can make a fort in it. I'm sure he'd let us." Jill was getting exited too.

"Oh crap!" Bobby yelled. "Mom told us to be home about a while ago! Come on. We'd better get home or we won't be coming out here for a long time cuz we'll be grounded!"

The four climbed down from their perches, gathered their belonging (minus their stringers that the skunks made off with) and ran all the way home.

Keep on loving one another as brothers and sisters.

Hebrews 13:1 NIV

CHAPTER FOUR

CHURCH GOIN'

"Good morning kids!" Mrs. Mason always seemed so happy to see her Sunday school class. "Today's lesson ties in with the sermon that Pastor Higgin gave today."

Jill started feeling a little uncomfortable since she hadn't really paid attention to what Pastor said this morning.

"It was about forgiveness, right?" Toni piped up.

Jill gave Toni a look of surprise. The two of them had been writing notes back and forth to each other during the sermon. Jill wondered how Toni knew what was being said, but she didn't.

"You're right Toni" replied Mrs. Mason. "I'm so glad you were able to come to church with Jill today. It's so good to see you!"

"Thanks, Mrs. Mason. I really like coming to church."

Toni's family didn't attend church very often. About the only times they went were on Christmas and Easter. So whenever Jill invited her, she jumped at the chance. For the most part she attended church about 2-3 times a month. Sometimes Russel would come too, but since Jan worked most Sunday mornings, it was Russel's chance to have the house to himself.

"Let's start with a prayer. Heavenly Father, thank you for bringing us all together today to learn about Your will for us. Help these bright students to thirst for more of Your word. In Jesus' precious name we pray, Amen."

The class echoed "Amen."

"Alright, let's get our work books out and start reading some verses on forgiveness. Let's go around the room and each one of you can read a verse and then tell us what you think it means. Tom, let's start with you."

"Colossians 3:13. Bear with each other and forgive one another if any of you has a grievance against someone. Forgive as the Lord forgave you." Tom read with ease. Well except for the word "grievance" but with a little help from Mrs. Mason, he made it through.

"So what do you think that means 'to have a grievance with someone', Tom?"

Tom thought for a minute and then replied, "If you're mad at someone?"

"That's right. And 'bearing with each other' means having patience with each other. Ok, Jill, it's your turn. Will you read the next one please?"

With a clear voice, Jill started the next verse from her workbook. "Ephesians 4:31-32. Get rid of all bitterness, rage and anger, brawling and slander, along with every form of malice. Be kind and compassionate to one another, forgiving each other, just as in Christ God forgave you." Jill paused a second and then asked, "What's malice?"

"That's a good question. Does anyone know what malice means?"

A long pause followed. Mrs. Mason continued, "Malice is when you say something bad about someone. Most of the time it isn't true or it's exaggerated to make it sound really bad. Either way, we shouldn't be saying things like that about others."

"So it's kinda like a lie?" another classmate, Trever asked

"Well, it might be true but it's just not very nice. Think of it as if you were trying to make someone look bad so you said things about them that didn't make them seem very nice. It might be a very small thing that they said or did at some time, but you make a big deal of it so it makes the person look worse than they really are."

"Kind of like gossip!" Annie, a very shy, but friendly classmate stated.

"Yes, a lot like gossip. Good job Annie!"

Annie blushed.

"Great job class! Let's go on to the next verse. Toni, I think it's your turn."

"Matthew 6:14-15. For if you forgive other people when they sin against you, your heavenly Father will also forgive you. But if you do not forgive others their sins, your Father will not forgive your sins." When Toni was finished reading she looked up, "Well that's pretty plain. You get what you dish out!" The class and Mrs. Mason chuckled.

"That's right, Toni! You can look at this one as forgiveness is as much for you as it is for the person who sinned against you. You don't want that lack of forgiveness hanging over your head. But be careful that you don't just say you forgive someone. God knows your heart. He knows if you really mean it when you say you forgive someone."

"What if the person you're forgiving doesn't care if you forgive them? What if they keep doing bad things to you?" Karen asked with a hint in her voice that she was thinking about someone in particular.

"Good question, Karen. Another verse in the Bible says we should forgive seventy times seven times." Mrs. Mason quoted.

"Holy Moly! That's a lot! I'd lose track after the first couple hundred!" Tom shouted.

"I think that's the whole point, Tom. Jesus said we should basically just keep forgiving people." Mrs. Mason explained.

"Is that what they mean by 'forgive and forget'?", Toni asked.

"Something like that, Toni. I had a pastor explain to me one time that it's more like 'forgive and let go.' It's almost impossible for us to completely forget when someone sins against us, especially if they keep doing it. But if we try our best to forgive them and not hang on to that hurt or anger, then our heavenly Father will see that and know we are really trying to forgive. Does that make sense?" A soft unanimous "Yeah" was heard from the class.

"You're doing great class. It sounds like you're really catching on to what the Bible is telling us about forgiveness. Let's go on to the next verse. Let's see, Toni had the last one so Annie I believe it's your turn."

In a barely audible voice, Annie started, "2 Corinthians 5:17, Therefore, if anyone is in Christ, the new creation has come: The old has gone, the new is here!"

"This is such great news! Do you know what this means?" Mrs. Mason said with such enthusiasm it got the whole class excited!

"That we get to start all over again, once we're forgiven?" Jason blurted out!

"Excellent, Jason! That's exactly what that means!" Mrs. Mason praised Jason, who now had his chest puffed out.

Tom leaned over and patted Jason on the back. "Way to go!" Tom continued with the praise. This of course made the class break out in laughter.

"This means that God doesn't hold our sins against us. We get to start all over again. Isn't that fantastic?" Mrs. Mason said as she looked at all the smiling faces of the kids in her class. "Are you sure you kids are only in 5th grade? You're awfully smart!"

Mrs. Mason had such a way to make everyone feel so good about themselves. It was no wonder the kids enjoyed coming to Sunday school.

"Ok, we better get on with the next ones. We're going to be pushing it on time to get through them all. Brian, I believe it's your turn."

Brian straightened up in his chair and began to read, "Psalm 103:12, As far as the east is from the west, so far has he removed our transgressions from us." Brian, being a bit of a class clown added, "What about from the north to the south."

To this he didn't get the response he was going for. Most of the kids just rolled their eyes and gave a moan. Mrs. Mason chuckled though. "Yes, from the north to the south as well. Mostly this is telling us that there's no length our God won't go to forgive our sins. Isn't that a comforting feeling to know that our heavenly Father wants to forgive us? He wants us to be forgiven as much as He wants us to forgive."

"Yeah, He's pretty cool like that." Brian tried again for a chuckle. This time he was a little more successful.

"Ok, Jason. It's your turn."

"Daniel 9:9 The Lord our God is merciful and forgiving, even though we have rebelled against him." Jason read. Then with a puzzled look on his face he asked, "Is sinning rebelling?"

"Well, it's going against what God has told us to do. When you go against what your parents ask you to do, isn't that rebelling?" Mrs. Mason posed the question to the class.

Jill added to the conversation, "I always thought of rebelling as a really crazy kind of going against what your parents want."

"Yeah, like being really snotty and talking back to them." Toni added.

"Or breaking the law." Jason continued. "That's really rebelling!"

"Yes, it is rebelling. It's all rebelling. God has set out rules for us to follow." Mrs. Mason posed yet another question to the class. "If we know it's not what God wants us to do, then isn't that rebelling against His rules?"

"Yup!" Tom replied.

This was followed by several more *"Yup's "*from the rest of the class. Just then the bell rang, telling them that Sunday school was done for the day.

"Well there's the bell. I just want to say before we pray that this has been one of the best conversations we've had and I'm so proud of all of you for your participation. Let's bow our heads and pray."

The class quieted down and bowed their heads.

"Heavenly Father." Mrs. Mason prayed. "Thank you for these wonderful students. Thank you for their loving hearts and sharp minds. Thank you for their willingness to hear your Word and work to understand it better. Guild them in the days to follow, to put these lessons to good use and follow Your will each and every day. In Your precious name we pray, Amen."

A unified "Amen" was spoken by the class. As they all got up and headed for the door, they yelled "Bye, Mrs. Mason!"

"See you next week kids!" Mrs. Mason returned.

As Toni and Jill walked past Mrs. Mason, Toni said with a hint of silliness, "I'll work on that not being a rebel, Mrs. Mason!"

"You do that Toni!" Mrs. Mason joked back. "Hope to see you next week."

Jesus overheard them and said, "I want little children to come to me, so never interfere with them when they want to come,"

Matthew 19:14 TPT

CHAPTER FIVE

FIGHT THE GOOD FIGHT

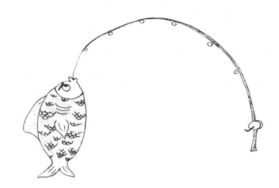

After the crazy outcome of the fishing excursion the Fab Four went on, Jill and Toni wanted to go fishing again, but this time by themselves. That swampy side of the pond seemed to be beckoning them to come try again. After all, they were having great luck...until the uninvited guests showed up, that is.

So they gathered the gear they needed, checked to make sure the boys weren't around and headed for the woods. With a constant eye out for the smelly intruders (the skunks, not their brothers), they made their way to the swampy side of the pond once again. Once settled in, they had a bite or two but nothing like the last trip.

Casting had always been a challenge for both of them. They were determined to get better at it so they could impress their brothers. During one cast, Jill caught Toni's cap and sent it sailing into the pond. Luckily she was able to reel it in. After all, it was Toni's favorite cap! Then Toni tried to cast so hard she threw her whole rod and reel into the water. As luck would have it, Jill was able to hook onto it and bring it in.

The girls were having lots of laughs and getting plenty of practice casting, when all of a sudden Toni's pole gave a couple of big tugs! As Toni set the hook she knew she had a real fighter on her line! She fervently worked to bring it in but this fish seemed to know what she was trying to do! And he wasn't having any part of it. Toni paced the shore line trying to tire out the whopper, but mostly it was Toni who was becoming tired. As she walked up and down the water's edge, she'd trip and fall down but Jill was right there to help her back up again.

The two of them seemed to know what the other was thinking because hardly a word was said. Yet they marched up and down the shoreline as if they had been practicing this scenario all their lives. The pacing went on for what seemed to be hours, but was really only a matter of minutes. The fish made its way to the fallen tree that was half in the water and half on the shore. Toni, determined to win this battle, headed out onto the log with Jill in tow. This fish knew just how to make it as difficult as possible for them to bring him in. It was at this point the young fishermen realize *they didn't have a net*! How on earth were they going to bring in this fish, and standing on a log no less? Before they had a chance to figure it out, KAPLOOSH!! Both girls were in the water!

A natural fighter instinct took over both the girls! They weren't about to give up on fighting this aquatic beast! With Toni pulling up on the rod and Jill grabbing for the fish, the battle ensued with the three of them jumping and splashing in the water. Then it finally happened! Jill was able to grab the tail as Toni held the rod up high. The two warriors dragged the still flopping fish up on the shore. It was the biggest fish either of them had ever seen! Once a safe distance on the shore the girls plopped down on the ground, exhausted. As they looked at each other, completely soaked, and now covered in mud, they burst out in side-splitting laughter. But by golly, they had their fish!

Without bothering to wash the mud off of themselves, they hauled their monstrous captive to the house to show off their trophy. As they came into the back yard, Levi, Bobby and Russel were playing catch in the yard. The boys were about to tease the girls about looking like a couple of cats that had fallen in the ditch water when they noticed the massive fish the girls were proudly carrying.

"Wow! Look at that monster fish!" Levi hollered! "That thing must weigh more than the two of you combined!"

"Isn't it a beauty?" Toni yelled back.

Just then Mrs. Turnbaugh came out the back door. "Oh my goodness! Look at you two!" clasping her face with her hands. "What happened to you girls?"

"We fought this fish until we won, Mom!" Jill exclaimed. "It was the most fun I've ever had fishing...or doing anything for that matter!" The girls, laughed in agreement!

"Well you need to go wash off. And YOU ARE NOT going into the house until you rinse the first layer of mud off of your bodies!" Mother used that 'I mean business' tone. "Use the garden hose to wash off as much of that mud as possible. Bobby, you and Russel take that fish and fillet it. We'll send it to the smoke house."

"But it's a carp! They're gross!" Bobby protested. "Besides, they caught it, they should have to clean it."

"Yes, I know it's a carp. That's why we're going to send it to the smoke house. The girls need to get cleaned up since it's getting late. Furthermore..."

This is where Bobby knew he had pushed his Mother too far with his complaining.

"It's what I told you to do, so get going!"

"Yes ma'am." Russel stepped in before Bobby's whining got them into trouble. "Come on. Let's go see how much this thing weighs!"

Bobby, still fussing about having to do the dirty work, followed Russel into the garage. By this time, Levi had the garden hose ready to spray the still beaming, mud-dripping, fishing champions off. The girls squealed as the cold water hit them!

"Oh my gosh! That's freezing!" they both screamed!

Two are better than one, because they have a good return for their labor: If either of them falls down, one can help the other up. But pity anyone who falls and has no one to help them up.

Ecclesiastes 4:9-10 NIV

CHAPTER SIX

DOING SOMETHING NICE FOR SOMEONE ELSE

Jan Owen never made a fuss about her own birthday. She did, however, like to make her family feel special on *their* birthdays. She had them decide what they wanted for supper, what they wanted to do on their birthday and of course she'd make them a yummy cake. And no matter what, she never worked on their birthdays.

It always made the family laugh when she would ask Russel what he wanted for his birthday. Year after year it was the same thing. Spaghetti for supper, Monopoly for the thing to do and a chocolate cake with cherry pie filling on the top.

John wasn't a whole lot better. For as long as anyone could remember, he wanted Pork chops for supper, watch the movie "Robin Hood" for the thing to do and a peach cobbler for his birthday "cake". The kids would give him a hard time about not being able to put candles in a peach cobbler. Their dad just laughed and said, "That's the whole point! I don't need to be reminded how old I am!"

Jan's birthday was coming up and this year Toni wanted to do something special for her Mother on *her* special day. Toni told Russel of her plan. She asked for some input on what to make, what to do and what to get her for a gift. Not having much of a knack for this type of thing, Russel was very little help. But Toni was determined to do something nice for her hardworking Mom. When her Dad got home that night, Toni tried to involve him in her plan as well. He, at least, was a little more helpful. John offered to do the grocery shopping for whatever Toni needed. That still left Toni to do the planning.

To the drawing board Toni went! She was trying to remember what the dish was that her Mom ordered the last time they were at a restaurant. It had chicken, bacon and pasta in it. Toni called Jill and asked her get on the computer to look up the recipe. Jill did as asked and found it.

"Chicken Carbonara" Jill reported. "This looks really yummy! Are you allowed to cook bacon though?"

"I might have to have Dad or Russel help me with that part." Even though Toni had some experience in the kitchen, she had never fried bacon before since it splattered so badly. "Print up the recipe for me would you, please? I'll have Dad get the stuff for it."

"What are ya gonna to make for dessert? Something chocolate?" Toni could see the gleam in Jill's eyes even over the phone.

"Oh you know it! Mom loves chocolate! Maybe that cake that you pour caramel over it while it's still warm?" Now Toni's eyes were gleaming as well!

"Ooooo, that sounds good! Let me know if you need any help." Jill offered. "I gotta go. I've got gymnastic practice in a little bit. I sure wish you'd join the team."

"I'm already in dance classes with you! I think that's plenty. Besides, I've got a birthday to take care of." Toni was glad to have an excuse so she wouldn't have to go through the 'Join the team' speech again from Jill.

"K! I sent the recipe to the printer. I'll bring it to school tomorrow. See ya!" Jill replied in a rush.

'Ok! There's two things down.' Toni thought to herself. *'Now to figure out what fun thing to do and what to get Mom for a gift.'*

It had been a few days since the entree and dessert had been decided. Toni was still having trouble with the last two pieces to the birthday party puzzle. While running errands with her Mom, they stopped at the hardware store. Toni liked shopping with her Mom. It gave them the one on one time they both craved.

"We need to get some oil for the lawn mower. If the bug spray is on sale we need some more of that too." Jan informed Toni.

As they walked through the store, collecting the items they needed, Jan spotted the pretty new planters the store just got in.

"Oh, look how pretty these are Toni!" Mother almost squealed as she headed toward the gardening section.

"Wow! Those are pretty." All of the sudden, it hit Toni! *'We can get Mom some of these pots and some plants for her birthday!'* Toni thought to herself. *'But what if she wanted to get them now? I've got to get her out of the store, quick!'*

As luck would have it, a friend of Jan's came by. The ladies started a conversation about something else besides the pretty planters. By the time they were done talking, Jan realized it was getting late.

"It's been great chatting Barb, but I've got groceries in the car and hungry kids to feed. I'd better be getting home. See you later!" Jan said good-by to her friend and headed to the counter with the two items they originally came for.

Toni was relieved! That crisis was adverted! As they were driving home, Toni had another idea. *'We could help Mom plant the new plants in the new pots and help her with the garden. It's something she likes to do and it's something we can all do together.'* Toni was feeling pretty good about her idea. She sat back in her seat with a big grin on her face.

"What are you all grins about, Missy?" Mom asked suspiciously.

'Oh no! Think fast!' Toni panicked for a second. "Nothing! Just glad to be going home."

Later that evening, Toni shared her plans with her Dad and brother, who both agreed these were great ideas.

'So there we have it!' Toni thought to herself. 'We'll have Chicken Carbonara and a salad for supper, Chocolate cake for dessert, and we'll buy the pretty pots and some plants and help Mom plant them.'

The next day, with permission from their parents, Jill and Toni walked uptown to get some supplies for a school project. Being the adventurous girls they are, a few other stores were investigated as well. They entered a clothing boutique that just recently opened. Jill, of course, being very fashion conscious was in heaven but even "tom-boy" Toni was mesmerized by the beautiful array of jewelry, hair clips, purses, scarves, hats and more. This store was completely different than any other store in town.

While Jill was being assisted by a store personnel, Toni gazed through the glass case that held all the marvelous little items. She spotted the most unique hair clip. It wasn't like some of the plastic clips that were next to it in the case. This one was made of metal, with swirling vines and little leaves. It was simple, yet elegant.

'Mom would love something like this' Toni thought. *'I wonder how much it cost.'*

There was only one attendant in the store, so Toni had to interrupt Jill from her futile attempt to make the employee think she was a fashionista. As Toni approached the two, she could tell the employee was getting a little annoyed with Jill, who by this time was making quite the spectacle of herself.

"Excuse me, but I didn't see any other people here to help me." Toni said in the most polite and grown up voice she could muster. "But there's something in the glass case over there that I'd like to look at."

Immediately the employee turned her attention to Toni, being grateful for the break from Jill's constant questions and fussing over the clothing.

"Yes, I'm afraid I'm the only one here for a little while yet." The employee replied. "What piece were you looking at?"

As Toni and the attendant walked over to the glass case they could hear the "Yeah, but..." from Jill being left behind.

"It's this hair clip with the leaves and vines." Toni explained. "Can you tell me how much it is?"

"Well let's see." As the attendant opened the case, "This one here?"

"Yes, that one."

"Let's see, the tag says $5."

"Perfect!" Toni was excited! That's just how much she had been saving up for something special. And this was definitely something special "I'll take it!"

"Would you like it gift wrapped? It's no extra charge."

"That would be great!" Toni was so excited! A beautiful gift and she didn't have to wrap it. Could this get any better?

"What are you getting?" Jill poked her head over Toni's shoulder.

"It's a gift for Mom. Isn't it pretty?"

"Wow! Look at you being all girly and everything. I must be rubbing off on you after all!"

Both of the girls giggled! What an adventure this afternoon had turned out to be for both of them.

May He give you the desire of you heart and make all your plans succeed.

Psalm 20:4 NIV

CHAPTER SEVEN

MANY HANDS MAKE LIGHT WORK

Jan's birthday surprise went off without a hitch! John Owen was home for a few days before the surprise party. He helped Toni as he said he would. Russel fried the bacon for the supper so Toni wouldn't get injured by the splattering bacon grease and even helped with the cleanup. Toni made the chocolate cake with the caramel sauce melted into it. She used whipped cream for the frosting and added colorful sprinkles to the top. She found a cake candle in the drawer to make it a perfect birthday cake.

A couple days before the party, the three of them went to the hardware store where Jan had admired the planters. They purchased three large pots, several colorful plants and a couple bags of potting soil. It was quite the challenge to keep these items hidden from Jan but they managed to pull it off.

When John went to the grocery store to purchase the items for the dinner and cake, he asked Jan's boss to let her go home early that day so they could have the afternoon to surprise her. Her boss was more than happy to play along with the plan!

As Jan came through the door that afternoon, the three of them yelled "Surprise!" Jan was so shocked she dropped her purse on the floor!

"Oh for heaven's sake! You three nearly gave me a heart attack!" Jan laughed. "What on earth is all this?"

"Happy birthday Mom!" Toni yelled while giving her mom a big hug.

"Happy birthday Mom!" Russel joined in on the hug.

"Happy birthday sweetheart." John joined in. "We, that is Toni, thought you needed a birthday party. Russel and I thought it was a good idea too."

Jan was overwhelmed with emotion. With tears rolling down her cheeks she said, "This is so sweet of you all. I've never had a birthday party before. Thank you so very much!"

"Let's eat! I'm starved!" Russel blurted out!

With lots of laughter, they all enjoyed an evening of celebration.

"So how did the party go last night?" Jill asked Toni as they headed into school.

Toni beamed "It was fantastic! The food turned out good, the cake was delicious and Mom really liked her flower pots. We sure made a mess with all that potting soil though!"

"What about the hair clip?" Jill was curious.

Still beaming, Toni said, "She loved it! She said I can borrow it any time I'd like."

"But you got it for her. Why would you use it too?" Jill looked completely appalled.

"We share a lot of things like that. It's no big deal."

"But you got it for her so you shouldn't be using it too. That's kind of selfish."

"No it's not! It's more practical this way."

As the bell rang the girls headed into class. Toni thought about what Jill said about being selfish.

'Jill just doesn't understand that we don't have the money to spend on buying lots of extra stuff like they do. Mom and I share lots of things so we don't have to spend so much money on things like that.'

That was one big difference between Toni and Jill. While Jill's family didn't think twice to spend money on frivolous items, Toni's family had to be more careful with their spending.

That afternoon, as Toni was walking home after school, she was still feeling pretty good about the night before. She remembered the astonished look on her Mom's face as they yelled 'Surprise!' and the tears that rolled down Jan's face as they all gathered around her. What a great evening that was.

Coming through the door, Toni heard her parents in the back of the house. Their voices were loud, at least her father's voice was loud. She could hear her mother saying things in reply to him. Toni couldn't make out what they were talking about. She stood still so she could hear them and not let them know she was there yet.

As they continued to argue she knew her father was upset about money. He was yelling about the bills and the money they were spending. She could hear her mother trying to calm him. Just then her father came through the door and saw Toni standing there.

"What's wrong? Why are you yelling at Mom?" Toni's voice was shaking.

"Nothing! Don't you have homework to do or something?" John barked at Toni.

"John, don't take it out on her." Jan intervened.

"Don't tell me how to talk to my own kid!" John snapped back.

With that Toni ran back out the door. It scared her when her Dad acted like this. She didn't know what to do or what to say. So she did what she always did when this happened. She went to Jill's house.

Later that evening, Jan drove over to the Turnbaugh's house and picked up both Toni and Russel who happened to be there too. The drive home was very quiet. As they pulled in the drive Toni noticed that her Dad's truck wasn't there. She felt relieved that he wasn't there to argue with her Mom any more, but sad that the happiness they experienced yesterday wasn't going to carry on into today. Since the kids ate supper at the Turnbaugh's they just went to their rooms, did their homework and went to bed.

The Lord is close to the brokenhearted and saves those who are crushed in spirit.

Psalm 34:18 NIV

CHAPTER EIGHT

GRATITUDE

"Toni, PLEASE!" Jill begged. "If you don't go with me, I'll be bored out of my mind!"

Jill's grandmother's birthday party was next weekend. Since her cousins were all older than her and she had nothing in common with them, she got bored easily at family functions. By recruiting Toni to go, Jill felt she'd have someone to talk to.

"Fine! Let me ask my mom and I'll let you know." Toni relented

"Awesome! It's next Saturday. We'll leave about 9 am. Wear that dress you wore for the Dance team banquet." Jill rattled off.

"A dress!" Toni yelled. "Are you kidding me? I've got to wear a dress?"

"Well you don't want to look underdressed, do you? You'll be fine." Jill continued to boss. "We just sit around anyways. It's not like we play games or anything fun."

By this time Toni was regretting considering the invitation. Toni thought to herself, *'With any luck, Mom will say I can't go'*

"Sure you can go, honey." Mom sounded so happy for Toni.

"Oh, ok." Toni's disappointment was obvious.

"I thought you'd be happy I said yes. What's up with this gloomy face?"

"Jill says I have to wear a dress."

Mom chuckled at her daughter's displeasure. "You'll be fine dear. It's a good thing to get dressed up every now and then." Jan reassured Toni. "I tell you what! You can borrow my hair clip that you bought me for my birthday."

Toni perked up a bit. "Really? You don't mind? I mean you haven't even had a chance to wear it yet."

"Absolutely!" Mom insisted. "What's mine is yours!"

"And what's mine is yours." Toni echoed.

"That's right. Remember, I borrowed your pretty scarf that you got for Christmas last year? Share and share alike. That's how we roll!"

Toni was feeling much better about this party now. She called Jill to give her the news. Toni had to move the phone away from her ear because of Jill's squeals of happiness!

"Ok, everyone! We'd better get going. It's an hour drive and we don't want to arrive late." Mr. Turnbaugh ordered. "You know how Grandma doesn't like tardiness."

Mrs. Turnbaugh was on her phone as she came out to the car. "Levi won't be joining us. He said he's got a last minute meeting to go to for his baseball league." Fran's voice gave her disappointment away. Everyone could tell she was very upset by this last minute announcement from her eldest son.

"Wow, that's the best he could come up with to get out of going!" Olivia spouted.

"That's enough Olivia." Mother snapped.

Listening to all of this, Toni was beginning to regret accepting this invitation. She thought, *'Just how bad is this Grandmother? It doesn't sound like anyone really likes to go. I wish I had my Grandma closer so we could just drive an hour to go see her. It wasn't always a fun visit to go see Grandma, but she was still her Grandma. It always made her very happy when we'd go to see her. And she's really sweet and tells funny stories.'* Toni was wishing she was going to her own Grandma's instead of Jill's Grandma's. As Jill and Toni were getting into the car, Fran stopped Toni.

"Don't you look lovely, Toni? It's nice of you to come with us so Jill will have someone to spend time with." Toni just smiled back.

"That's a beautiful hair clip you have." Fran continued

"Thank you. Miss Fran. It's my Mom's." Toni replied

As Toni climbed in the car, Jill said "Isn't that the clip you gave your Mom for her birthday?"

"Yup."

"And now you're wearing it?"

"Yeah."

"Isn't that kind of tacky to give someone a gift and then you use it yourself?" Jill was showing her catty side.

"She said I could wear it. What's the big deal?" Toni was on the defense now.

"I would just never give someone a gift and then use it myself."

"Whatever."

Toni knew that Jill has no sense of sharing. Jill had always been able to have her own nice things. She didn't understand that Toni and her family didn't live the same life style as the Turnbaughs. They've had to learn to share what they have.

As they pulled up to Grandma's house Toni scoped out the whole scene. There were 3 cars in the drive that led up to a very nice looking house. The yard was big with lots of flowers and a bench under a gazeebo.

'So far, doesn't look too scary.' Toni thought to herself.

"Alright, everybody out!" Nash commanded with a laugh.

"Bobby, will you take the casserole into the kitchen please?" Fran instructed. "Oh, well I see Olivia has already found her cousins, so Jill will you take Grandma's present in to her please?"

"K." Jill moaned.

"And it wouldn't hurt to put a smile on your face either. It's a birthday party after all. Not a funeral." Fran looked sternly into the face of her youngest.

"Yes ma'am." Jill returned with a forced smile.

As the girls walked toward the house, Toni overheard Fran say to Nash. "That girl is getting a real attitude lately."

"She'll be alright." Nash, was always quick to come to his kids' defense. "Having Toni here will help."

As Jill and Toni walk through the door a woman's voice was heard above the commotion inside the house. "Oh there's my girl! Hi sweetheart. I'm so happy to see you!"

"Hi Grandma." Jill answered.

Toni was surprised at how nice Jill's Grandma looked. After the way they all talked she expected someone who resembled the Wicked Witch of the West. Not this sweet, happy lady that came over and gave Jill a hug and a kiss.

"And who do we have here?" Grandma continued.

"This is my friend Toni." Jill made the introductions.

"Well Toni it's wonderful to finally meet you. I've heard so much about you over the years. I'm so glad you could join us today." Grandma said in a very welcoming way.

Bashfully Toni replied, "Hi. Happy birthday."

"Well thank you dear!" Grandma responded, giving Toni a warm smile that made her feel very welcomed.

"Happy birthday, Mother!" Nash announced coming in behind the girls.

"Come on. Let's go downstairs." Jill pulled Toni's arm.

"What's downstairs?"

"It's what's NOT downstairs. It's where we can get away from all of this!" Jill stated in a haughty tone.

Toni just couldn't figure out what Jill's problem was. The house was nice, there were people around but they all seemed to be busy talking to each other, and Jill's Grandma seemed very nice. So why was Jill acting so aloof? Maybe time would tell.

The girls had been watching a movie when someone yelled downstairs to them. "Lunch is ready!"

Jill rolled her eyes and said, "Well, we'd better go or they'll come down to get us."

As the girls emerged from the basement, Jill's Grandma said, "Well there you two are. I was wondering where you disappeared to. Are you hungry? There's enough food to feed an army out there."

The three walked out to the dining room where the table was set up buffet style. Nash came up behind his mother. "Here Mom, how about I hold a plate for each of us and you dish up what you want."

"Sounds like a plan." Grandma answered with a smile.

The food looked so good. Toni couldn't think of when she had seen this much food before. Since she was a bit nervous about the trip she hadn't eaten much for breakfast, so she was really hungry.

"Don't forget to save room for cake and ice cream!" Grandma reminded everyone.

After two trips to the buffet along with cake and ice cream, Toni was stuffed!

"Ok everyone, it's time to open gifts!" Fran declared. "Girls will you go get the gifts and bring them over to Grandma please?

"Wow! That's a stack of presents!" quietly Toni declared.

"I know! We'll have to make lots of trips." Jill answered.

Grandma opened her gifts and thanked each person individually. Afterwards, everyone just chatted amongst themselves.

Toni noticed Olivia and Bobby were sitting by Grandma, chatting about school, sports and whatever events were happening in their lives. Fully expecting to go sit with them, Jill instead pulled on Toni's arm once again and said, "Come on. Let's go finish that movie."

"Don't you want to talk to your Grandma?" Toni questioned.

"No, that's boring!" Jill snapped.

In a couple of hours, Fran called down to the girls, "Time to go girls!"

"Just a few more minutes. The movie's almost done." Jill replied.

"You've got about 15 minutes. Then come say good-bye to Grandma."

Toni was feeling very uncomfortable that they hadn't spent any time with Jill's Grandma or anyone else for that matter.

As the girls started up the stairs, it seemed a lot quieter. Toni realized that almost everyone had already left.

Jill went up to her Grandma and gave her a hug. "Bye Grandma."

"Bye sweetheart. Sorry we didn't get to visit much this trip."

"Yeah." Jill said as she turned to leave.

"Toni, it was very nice to finally meet you." Grandma said as she put an arm around Toni's shoulder.

"I'm glad to meet you too. I hope you had a good birthday." Toni said doing her best to use her manners her parents taught her.

"Yes, it was very nice. I hope you'll come with Jill's family again when they come back to visit."

This made Toni feel very welcomed and kind of like being part of the family. She smiled at Grandma and said, "I'd like that."

As they pulled into town Bobby shouted, "Hey let's stop at the Chicken Shack! I'm starved!"

"Ooo! That sounds so good right now!" Olivia agreed with her brother.

"But that's only for when we are coming back from a game." Jill loved their tradition of stopping to get chicken strips from the Chicken Shack.

"I guess we could. That way I don't have to make supper." Fran chuckled.

"Chicken Shack it is then!" Nash announced.

They ordered their food to eat there. Toni was with the Turnbaugh's many times during their trips to various sporting events. Usually her brother Russel was with them, so she knew she was going to have to rub it into him that he missed out on their favorite chicken strips.

After supper, the Turnbaugh's dropped Toni off at her house.

"Thanks for taking me with to Grandma's house and thanks for the chicken strips!" Toni shouted as she climbed out of the car.

"You're welcome!" Mr. and Mrs. Turnbaugh replied in unison.

Later, Jill called Toni.

"You forgot your sweater in the car. I'll bring it to school tomorrow."

"Oh, thanks. I forgot I even brought it." Toni chuckled. "That was a nice party. The food was really good."

"Yeah, there's always a ton of it."

"How come you didn't want to talk to anyone?" Toni couldn't help but ask.

"They're boring. Plus Olivia and my cousins always act so snotty to me. They treat me like a baby.'

"What about your Grandma? You hardly spoke to her."

"It's no big deal. We don't see her as much as we do my Mom's family, so I really don't know this Grandma as much."

"Well you're not going to get to know her if you don't at least try." Toni blurted out. It made Toni feel kind of sorry for Jill's Grandma.

"Whatever." was all Jill said in reply.

Even a child makes himself known by his acts, by whether his conduct is pure and upright.

Proverbs 20:29 KJV

CHAPTER NINE

HONESTY IS THE BEST POLICY

"Turnbaugh, what are you doing?" Phil yelled.

"Trying to find a big flat rock!" Levi yelled back. "Here's one."

Levi hefted the large, flat rock and carried it to the bridge where he and some friends had been throwing rocks into the water below.

The large rock made a loud 'SPLAT' sound as it hit the water.

"Wow, that was cool!" they all yelled

This is what Levi was doing while his family had gone to visit their Grandmother. He made up the story about having a coaches meeting so he could stay home. Hanging out with his friends had become more important to Levi than what it should be. The past 6 months, Levi and his friends had chosen a very unwise path. They started smoking marijuana. Levi's grades had started to decline. His interest in school had diminished, and his interest in his family had diminished as well.

Ever since the shoulder injury a couple of years ago, that ended his ability to play sports, Levi's attitude had been getting worse. The once "A" student was now a struggling "B" student at best. The respectful young man had become very belligerent with authority figures. It didn't help that whenever he got into any sort of trouble, his parents would bail him out. Now it was almost like he was trying to see just how far his parents would go to keep his misbehaviors out of the public eye. Up until now, most of what Levi had done wasn't actually illegal.

"I gotta get home." Phil said after throwing one more rock in the water.

"What time is it?"

"It's almost 6." Answered Jim.

"Crap! I'd better get home too!" Levi chimed in. "I told my Mom I had a coach's meeting so I wouldn't have to go to my Grandma's birthday party."

"Hummm, going to Grandma's or getting high with us. I think you made a good call on that one!" Phil mocked.

"Yeah, this is a lot more fun!" Levi returned.

That Sunday, Toni went to church with Jill again.

"Good morning kids!" Mrs. Mason greeted her Sunday school class. Our lesson today is on Honesty. But first, let's start with a word of prayer."

Everyone folded their hands and bowed their heads.

"Heavenly Father, thank you for bringing all these wonderful students here today to learn more about Your Word. Bless them with open minds, open hearts and a desire to know more about You. Amen."

In unison, the class echoed the Amen.

"Let's get our workbooks out and see what interesting things it has for us to discover today!" Mrs. Mason instructed.

The class read 1 John 3:18 and Proverbs 6:16-20 and discussed their meanings. Then Mrs. Mason told the story of Zacchaeus and Jesus.

She explained, "Zacchaeus was a tax collector. That wasn't a very honest profession back then. Many tax collectors did things that were dishonest and sometimes kept some of the tax money they collected for themselves. But Jesus saw the good in Zacchaeus and said he wanted to have supper with him at Zacchaeus' house! This really upset some of the village people. They couldn't believe Jesus would make friends with someone like Zacchaeus! But after Jesus and Zacchaeus had supper and had a chance to talk, Zacchaeus had a change of heart. He promised he would give half of his possessions to the poor and repay the people 4 times what he had taken from them. Zacchaeus not only saw the error of his ways but he no longer wanted to live that kind of life. He wanted to be honest and follow Jesus' ways. This made Jesus very happy and He said, 'Today salvation has come to this house, because this man, too, is a son of Abraham. For the Son of Man came to seek and to save what was lost.' Zacchaeus was lost in his dishonesty but was now found in his repentance. Isn't that a wonderful story?"

"Just like that, Jesus forgave him for stealing all that money?" Tom asked.

"That's right. Zacchaeus was truly sorry for what he did and did something to make it right." Answered Mr. Mason.

With suspicion in his voice Trever asked. "What if he was just saying that to make Jesus think he had changed?"

"Do you think he could have fooled Jesus? Remember, Jesus knows what's in our hearts." Mrs. Mason responded. "Let's continue with some more Bible passages. Toni will you read James 1:26 please? "

Toni fumbled to find her place in the workbook, cleared her throat and began. "Those who consider themselves religious and yet do not keep a tight rein on their tongues deceive themselves, and their religion is worthless."

"That kind of goes along with your question Trever. Just because we say things to make it sound like we're sorry, doesn't mean we are following what the Bible says. Or saying things that are mean or not true and then say, 'Oh I'll just ask for forgiveness later and it'll be alright', that's not acting the way God wants us to, is it?"

"Is that being a hippocrate?" Karen stumbled with her wording.

A muffled chuckle came from a few students.

"I think you mean hypocrite, Karen. And yes, in some ways that person would be a hypocrite. Mostly it makes that person a deceiver. They're mostly deceiving themselves. If they think they are following what God has instructed us to do, yet do things that are dishonest or hurtful, then they aren't following Gods will very well. Jill, will you read Proverbs 10:9 please?"

Jill nervously shifted in her seat, found the passage and began. "Whoever walks in integrity walks securely, but whoever takes crooked paths will be found out."

"So is the crooked path the lying?" Karen asked

"Exactly!" Mrs. Mason answered "Good job Karen."

"Sounds pretty simple to me." Jill snorted. "Just don't lie and you'll be fine."

"Well, in some ways it is pretty simple. But when we listen to the sneaky snake, what happens?" Mrs. Mason asked.

"We get kicked out of the garden!" Tom shouted

Chuckles exploded from the class!

"That's right, Tom!" Mrs. Mason responded back.

The bell could be heard down the hallway.

"Wow! Class time sure went by quickly today! Let's pray before I dismiss class."

Everyone again folded their hands and bowed their heads.

"Heavenly Father, thank you for another wonderful class today. Help these young people to keep in mind what we've learned today about being honest and following Your Word. In Jesus precious name, Amen."

After a chorus of "Amen" the class jumped up and headed for the door.

"Have a great week everyone!" Mrs. Mason almost had to shout to the students since they were out the door in a flash.

"Bye Mrs. Mason!" Toni shouted over her shoulder as she went out the door.

So discard every form of dishonesty and lying so that you will be known as one who always speaks the truth, for we all belong to one another.

Ephesians 4:25TPT

CHAPTER TEN

HARD TIMES

"John, what are you doing home? Jan was startled to see her husband walk through the door several days before he was expected back. "Is everything alright?"

The look on John's face answered her question. Something was definitely not alright.

"I've really messed up Jan." John said with a great heaviness. "I got fired."

"Oh no! What happened?"

"I lost my temper. I got into an argument with Troy, the new guy. Things got out of hand and I broke some equipment. Mr. Nelson was there and fired me on the spot. I'm so sorry Jan. I don't know what's happening to me lately. My temper is getting worse and worse."

Seeing the anguish in her husband's face was breaking Jan's heart. "I know we've talked about this before and you didn't want to, but maybe it's time you seek some help to deal with your temper." The support Jan was showing was almost too much for John to handle.

His voice quivered as he looked at his wife. "As soon as I find another job, I promise I'll get some help."

"Until then we'll just cinch our belts up a little tighter." Jan was trying to be as positive as possible. Even though they were on a pretty tight budget the way it was, her mind was already thinking of ways they could cut back.

"Why don't you go get washed up. I'll make you a sandwich and then you can start looking for that new job."

"I don't know why you put up with me Jan. I really don't."

"Because I love you. You're a good man. God's leading you to something John. You just need to get right with Him and then things will start to fall into place."

John wrapped Jan in a big hug. She could feel him silently sob.

A couple weeks after John lost his job, he announced to his family, "Well it took me a little longer than I'd wanted but I got a new job!"

"That's great!" Russel shouted

"That's wonderful!" Jan joined in. "Where at?"

"At the Olsen ranch. I start tomorrow." John went on. "They're giving us a house to live in too. So I'm afraid that means we'll have to move. The pay is a lot less than I was making before so the free rent helps to make up for that."

With a look of panic, Toni asked, "We have to move?"

"I'm afraid so sweetie." Toni's father answered as gently as possible.

Toni was trying to be as understanding as possible. In the 2 weeks since her Dad lost his job, she had given up dance class and didn't get the new hoodie that she had been wanting. It was her way of helping to save money.

The rest of the family did things to help as well. Jan traded her nice SUV for a smaller, more economical car. She also took even more hours at work. Russel started a job on the weekends at the local car wash.

Something that Toni hadn't told her family about was the way Jill had been treating her lately. Ever since Toni quit the dance team, Jill was acting as if it was an embarrassment for her, not Toni. Some of the kids at school were taking notice to what was going on with Toni's family as well. Comments had been made to Toni about her family getting a different car, her brother getting a job and now Toni was sure they'd have something to say about them moving.

"Can we go see the house?" Jan was feeling a little apprehensive about moving into a house she had never been in before. "Do you know how many bedrooms it has?"

"Yup. Mr. Olsen said we can come out there anytime. It's empty right now and he gave me a key. How about we go out after supper?"

Supper was a bit tense. Everyone seemed to be thinking about moving. Each one of them had their own questions and apprehensions about moving but no one wanted to voice them just yet.

John was feeling several different emotions. He was grateful for a new job, but feeling guilty for losing his other one. He could see his wife and children weren't very happy about having to move. As all of these emotions stirred up in him, John was trying very hard to contain his temper. He thought his family would be a little more grateful that he found a new job. He was also thinking of his promise he made to his wife about going to a counselor once he found a job. This gave him even more stress because he knew counselors aren't cheap.

"Russel, I believe it's your turn to do dishes tonight." Jan interrupted the silence. "Toni, do you have any homework to finish?"

"No, since it's the end of school, we're just doing a bunch of studying for the tests. I studied earlier." Toni answered her Mother.

"Ok, well then how about you help your brother so we can go look at the house before it gets dark?" Mother instructed.

Toni just rolled her eyes. She wasn't very happy about having to help with the dishes since it wasn't her turn. Though sensing the tension in her Mother's voice she didn't protest.

With the table cleared, left overs stored, dishes washed, dried and put away, the family got into the little car and drove out to see their new house.

"How many miles is it from town?" Jan was concerned how long her drive would be each day to go to work.

"The house is 10 miles out and the area that I'll be working in is about 15." John answered.

The Olsen ranch was the largest ranch in the area. They raised milk cows, goats, a small heard of steers, an even smaller heard of pigs and a very large variety of poultry. Along with the livestock, they farmed several different crops. They were well known and well respected in the community. The ranch employed a couple dozen people and were known to be good employers.

As they pulled into the driveway, they could see the house. It looked like something out of a Norman Rockwell painting. The white two-story house had a porch on the front of it. Large trees were on all sides of it and one of them had a tire swing hanging from its large branch.

"Well, so far it looks very nice." Jan was trying to keep the mood positive. "How long has it been empty?"

"From what I was told the other hand just left about 3 days ago. He got promoted to the other part of the ranch."

"Oh that's good. It hasn't been empty for a long time."

Once in the house, the tension seemed to decline a bit. It was a very nice house. It was clean, well taken care off, spacious and had lots of windows. Toni and Russel were relieved when they saw a dishwasher in the kitchen.

The Lord hears His people when they call to Him for help. He rescues them from all their troubles. The Lord is close to the brokenhearted; He rescues those whose spirits are crushed.

Psalm 34:17-18 NLT

CHAPTER ELEVEN

DEAL WITH IT

"Ten miles! You may as well be in another country!" Jill wasn't taking the news about Toni's family moving very well.

"It's a really pretty house. Plus it has a dishwasher!" Toni was trying to think of something to make Jill feel better.

"I can't believe this is happening to me! First you have to quit the dance team and now you have to move. This is just so embarrassing!" The drama in Jill's voice was strong.

"It's not that big of a deal. I'm not embarrassed. It's just going to be a little different."

"Well you should be embarrassed. I mean, first your Dad loses his job, then you have to buy that tiny little car and now you have to move. What are the kids at school going to say?"

Now the indignation in Jill's voice was a little more than Toni could handle.

"I don't know why you're getting so upset. I really don't care what others say." Now it was Toni's turn to sound indignant.

"Well you should care! I was just starting to really make friends with the popular kids in school. We were getting invited to some of their parties and everything."

"Wow, I've never noticed what a snob you've become." Toni had had enough. "Sorry my family having some problems has caused you such embarrassment. If I'm such an embarrassment to you, why don't you just go hang out with your *POPULAR* friends?"

"Well maybe I will!"

With that, the two girls went their different ways.

"Jill, you're friends with Toni Owen, right?" Bethany, and a few other girls from the gymnastics team were talking before practice began.

In almost a whisper Jill replied, "Yeah, kind of."

"So what's going on with her? Kristen just told me she dropped out of dance." Then Lyndsey piped in, "Plus they moved too." "Are her parents getting divorced?" Bethany added. The questions came at Jill faster than she could think of what to say.

"I'm not really sure. We really don't talk much anymore. We just don't have much in common anymore." Jill was trying to sound as grown up as possible.

"I know what you mean. When I was younger, there were some kids I stopped hanging out with because they just didn't like the same things as me." Now Karen was trying to act grown up too.

Now, feeling like she was being accepted by her new friends, Jill continued the conversation.

"Yeah, Toni's family is just kind of different. I mean, she didn't understand the way normal people do things. Like when she bought her mother a hair clip as a gift, then Toni wore it herself!"

"Really? That's kind of tacky!" Kristen added into the conversation.

Now feeling like she was on a roll with making herself look good in her new friend's eyes, Jill continued to put Toni down.

"My family always felt sorry for her family so we'd take them places with us. But that's just the way my family is."

Jill was really laying it on thick now. It was as if she couldn't stop herself. As long as the other girls would listen, Jill continued. It made her feel superior and important.

A couple of weeks had passed since Toni and Jill last spoke. Toni was hurt that Jill didn't seem to care how all of these changes had affected her. Jill was more concerned with her reputation as a socialite than to think about her lifelong friend.

There was plenty of talk at school as to why Toni's family had changed so many things. Some of the girls from the dance team made comments around Toni that weren't very nice. They never said anything to her face but they always made sure it was loud enough so Toni could hear.

For the most part, Toni didn't pay much attention to them. What really hurt was that her best friend had turned her back on her when she needed her the most. Things were a little strained at home and Toni could use a friend to talk to.

As her father had promised, when he got a new job he would go to a counselor for his anger issues. On top of their other bills, now they had the added financial strain of paying for a counselor. On top of everything else, one of the girls who made it her business to make fun of Toni, lived right across from the counselor's office. She saw Toni's Dad going into the building a few times. So she felt it was her duty to share this information with the rest of her friends. This of course mortified Jill. The embarrassment was almost more than she could stand.

———————————————————————

While Jill was at Sunday school, Mrs. Mason asked her why Toni hadn't been coming to class with her lately. In Jill's new found bluntness, she replied, "It's just too embarrassing to hang out with her anymore." In Mrs. Mason's usual kind manner she reminded Jill that Jesus had dined with sinners. To that Jill coldly said, "Yeah, but Jesus didn't have to go to school and be around all the gossip and teasing!" As Jill walked away, Mrs. Mason just shook her head and said a silent prayer for both the girls.

As Bobby and Jill walked out to the car after church, Bobby asked Jill if she was going to go fishing with Russel, Toni and him later that day.

"I don't think so. I've got better things to do. I'm going over to Karen's house." The attitude was very obvious in Jill's voice.

"What's gotten into you lately? You've become a real snob." Bobby's attitude was equally as obvious.

"I'm not a snob! I just like other things now."

"Whatever! Ever since the Owens moved you stopped hanging out with Toni. And a lot of my friends at school say you're spreading gossip about Toni. That's just really crappy of you Jill. You should be standing by her now when she needs a friend. Where's your loyalty?"

"Leave me alone! Whatever is being said about the Owen family isn't gossip, it's true! And I don't want to be mixed up in it."

At school when Toni and Jill passed in the hallway, Toni smiled at Jill. Jill started to smile back but then was worried someone might see her so she just turned her head and pretended she didn't see Toni.

A few days later, while Toni was entering the girl's restroom, Jill was finishing washing her hands. Toni took the opportunity to say something that had been on her mind for a while.

"Hey Jill." Toni started the conversation.

"Hey." Jill's reply was almost silent.

"Jill, I just want you to know that I forgive you for the way you've been acting lately. I understand that it's really hard for you to accept everything that's happened."

Jill whipped around to face Toni. "I don't need your forgiveness! I haven't done anything wrong! Maybe you should save your forgiveness for your dad. He's the one that screwed everything up!" With that, Jill stormed out the door.

As Jill walked down the hallway an explosion of reasons were running through her head why she didn't need to be forgiven. Especially by someone in Toni's position.

Toni, on the other hand, was still standing there, a bit shocked that someone she had once called her best friend, just yelled at her like that. Then she remembered what Mrs. Mason said about forgiveness. "Forgiveness is for the one doing the forgiving more than the one needing forgiveness." While it still stung badly to have Jill speak to her like that, she was glad she tried to give Jill her forgiveness. Mrs. Mason was right. It did make Toni feel better.

Live happily together in a spirit of harmony, and be as mindful of another's worth as you are your own. Don't live with a lofty mind-set, thinking you are too important to serve others, but be willing to do menial tasks and identify with those who are humble minded. Don't be smug or even think for a moment that you know it all.

Romans 12:16 TPT

CHAPTER TWELVE

A HEALING TIME

As John Owen walked up to the Mental Health Clinic for the fourth visit, he was feeling like something was about to happen. His sessions with Mrs. Janes had been going better than he thought they would.

They had talked a great deal about the hostile family life John had been raised in. They talked about how important John's wife and children are to him. They talked about ways for John to deal with problems without letting his temper get out of hand.

In fact, John was able to put this into action at work one day. When he got home that night he told his wife and kids about how he stepped back and put himself in the other person's shoes. This gave him the chance to understand why the other guy was acting the way he was. So instead of John yelling back at his coworker, he just calmly walked away. John said that later on, this coworker came up to him and apologized for yelling at John.

"Great job, Dad!" Russel was beaming with pride for his father.

"You kind of did what I did to Jill, Dad. You forgave that guy! Forgiving others feels pretty good, huh Dad?" Toni's enthusiasm lit up the room.

"You know, you're right, sweetheart. It did feel good to forgive him." The shocked look on John's face was evident.

Today, though, John couldn't shake the feeling that something special was about to happen in his counseling session. It gave John a sense of pride to see how impressed his family was with his new found attitude.

Mrs. Janes sat across from John in her modest, yet comfortable office. She asked John how his week went. John told her about the altercation with his coworker and how good it felt to not lose his temper. Mrs. Janes was very pleased with his progress. John continued to tell her about what Toni had said. What struck him was the maturity of his young daughter. How happy it had made her to forgive her friend. John felt a little confused about forgiveness. He always thought forgiveness was something a priest gave to people, not what people gave to each other.

Mrs. Janes asked John if he went to church now or as a child. John explained how his family went to church a little, while he was growing up but he never felt anything special about it.

"Do you feel it might be something you'd like to pursue?" Mrs. Janes inquired.

"I've thought about it a few times. I knew a guy who went to church and we talked a little about it. My daughter goes with a friend of hers. Well, she used to until they had a falling out."

"Well if you're ever curious enough to follow up on it, I'd like to invite you to the church I attend. It's pretty laid back, no dress code or anything like that."

"Yeah, I'm not one to get all dressed up." John chuckled. "I can't believe I'm saying this but it sounds like something I'd like to try."

Mrs. Janes wrote the address on a piece of paper and handed it to John. "Here's the address and the time service starts. I think you'll like Pastor Jerry."

After John finished his session he walked out of the building with a feeling of excitement. He didn't understand why he felt that way, he just knew he felt excited about the future.

When John got home he told Jan about his session with Mrs. Janes. He showed her the piece of paper with the name and address of the church.

"Wow! I never thought I'd ever hear you say you wanted to go to church." Jan felt completely caught off guard by her husband's statement that evening.

"I know! I'm pretty shocked myself." John couldn't explain his feelings any better to his wife.

That next Sunday, the Owen family found themselves sitting in church. Music was playing from a 6 piece band. The music wasn't anything like what they thought would be playing in a church. It was upbeat, a bit loud and everyone seemed to be enjoying it. The words to the songs were shown on TVs mounted by the ceiling so everyone could see. After a few songs, announcements were shared about what was going on during the coming weeks. An offering was taken. John was glad he had a few dollars in his billfold. The kids were dismissed to Sunday school but Toni and Russel decided to stay with their parents.

As Pastor Jerry began to speak, it felt like he was talking one on one with everyone. Members of the congregation spoke out loud in agreement every now and then. There was laughter when the pastor would make a joke. There were a few "amens" spoken out loud in agreement with what was being said. All of this made John feel very comfortable. He listened intently to what the pastor was talking about.

The theme of the sermon was God's peace. Pastor read John 14:27, "Peace I leave with you; my peace I give you. I do not give to you as the world gives. Do not let your hearts be troubled and so, do not be afraid." He went on to read another passage. This time it was John 16:33 "I have told you these things, so that in me you may have peace. In this world you will have trouble. But take heart! I have overcome the world."

John couldn't get over the feeling that those passages were meant just for him. He thought it was a funny coincidence that they came from a book in the Bible that bore his name.

Towards the end of the service, Pastor Jerry asked if there was anyone who felt they were in need of some special prayers. He said, "If the Holy Spirit is moving and you to want to come up here, we can pray for you. So please feel free to just come up."

A few people started to make their way up to the front. The piano player started playing some soft music. And then it happened. John had this uncontrollable urge to go up there and be prayed for. At first he resisted the feeling.

'No! I can't go up there.' John thought to himself. 'What will people think? What will my family think? What will it feel like?' John couldn't move. 'But something is telling me this is the right thing to do. I want to feel more of what I've been feeling this morning.' The words were like something fighting inside of John's head. The next thing John knew, he was walking up to the front!

There were what Pastor called his "Prayer Warriors" up there praying with the people who had come up ahead of John. As John approached the front a man and a woman stood by his side. They greeted him kindly and the three of them started to pray together.

The feeling was overwhelming, indescribable and yet so very right. John asked God to come into his life and help him with his family. As for John's family, they were still sitting in the pew. A look of disbelief was on each one of their faces. Jan didn't even try to hide the tears of joy that were rolling down her cheeks.

When John returned to his seat, he looked at his family. Something seemed different. The look on Jan's face beamed with pride for her husband. The look on his children's faces were something he had never seen before. They had a look of respect. Respect for their father who just did something so brave, so out of character and so real.

My son, pay attention to what I say; turn your ear to my words. Do not let them out of your sight, keep them within your heart; for they are life to those who find them and health to one's whole body.

Proverbs 4:20-22 NIV

CHAPTER THIRTEEN

LEARN FROM YOUR MISTAKES

"I swear, officer, it's not mine!" Levi pleaded with the police officer who found a small bag of marijuana in the car that Levi was driving.

"Well I'm afraid I'm going to have to take you to the station." Officer Jacobs was trying to give Levi the benefit of the doubt since it wasn't Levi's car that he was driving. "I just can't let it go this time Levi."

At the Police Station, Levi called his father. Nash was at the station within 5 minutes. After speaking to Officer Jacobs in the other room, the two men emerged from the conference.

"Like I said, Mr. Turnbaugh, I can't let this go with just a warning. Even though the car doesn't belong to Levi, I still have to give him a ticket for speeding. We'll investigate the possession of a controlled substance and get back to you." Officer Jacobs was trying to be considerate of the situation and who he was talking to.

This wasn't the first time Levi had been in trouble. Mr. Turnbaugh usually came into the Police Station and smoothed things over with a promise that it wouldn't happen again and reminded them that he's donated a great deal of money to the community. Before this time the problems were small offenses. But possession of a controlled substance wasn't a small offenses and the Police Department was cracking down on the rising drug problem in their little town.

"So can I take my son home then Officer?"

"Here Levi, you need to sign this ticket and then yes, you can leave." Officer Jacobs was trying to be as polite as possible since he knew Mr. and even Mrs. Turnbaugh were known for pitching a bit of a fit whenever Levi got into any trouble.

"Levi, you're going to have to straighten up! This is serious!" Nash Turnbaugh was reading Levi the riot act once they got home.

"But it wasn't my pot!" Levi was trying to defend himself.

"Well then maybe you need to stop hanging around with those other kids! They're just going to get you into trouble with their pot smoking and whatever else they're doing."

"I agree with your father, Levi dear." Mrs. Turnbaugh spoke up trying to calm the situation. "I've always thought those boys were just troublemakers. It was so nice when you were friends with the Mason boy. Or what about Johnny Litner. He was always such a nice boy. Why don't you hang out with them anymore?"

"I don't know. Ever since I had to go off of the baseball team, I just don't seem to have much in common with them." Levi knew if he mentioned being injured and having to leave the baseball team, it would make his mother sympathize with him.

"That was a close one! I told the cops that my car had sat unlocked and the windows were down and that must have been how the bag of pot got in there" Phil and Levi had met up after things had cooled off with the police and most importantly, their parents.

"Yeah, I'm pretty sure I'll just have the speeding ticket out of the whole thing. My dad talked to Jacobs for a while. That usually smooths things over. I'm really mad though that I lost that bag of pot. I had a guy that wanted to buy it."

"Yeah, my mom went down there and got my car back." Phil didn't seem very upset about the whole incident either.

"Guess I'll just have to call my supplier again and get some more."

A week later, Levi had more pot to sell and was feeling pretty confident this time that he wouldn't get caught again. But that's not how things turned out for Levi.

While driving his own car, going from one house to the next, Levi didn't realize the police were following him. This time Levi's parents weren't going to be able to get him out of trouble.

If we boast that we have no sin, we're only fooling ourselves
and are strangers to the truth.

1 John 1:8 TPT

CHAPTER FOURTEEN

<u>SCARY DECISIONS CAN BE GREAT!</u>

Several days after John Owen had walked up to the front of the church and accepted Jesus Christ into his life, the Owen family were still talking about it.

"So are we going back to church again on Sunday?"

"Do they have a Sunday School?"

"I wonder if we know any of the kids that go to that church."

"I saw a couple of kids there that I know."

Toni and Russel were spouting out questions faster than Mr. and Mrs. Owen could gather their thoughts to answer them.

"I'd like to go back there." John snuck in a statement.

"I'd really like to go back too." Jan agreed with her husband.

"Are you going to go back up to the front again Dad?" Toni had a bit of a giggle to her question.

"I think that was a onetime deal, Toni." Her Dad replied with a bit of a giggle himself.

"Although to see those looks on your faces again, it might be worth it!" John was mimicking the look of surprise he saw as he came back to the pew.

Everyone got a good laugh. Even though no one said anything at the moment, all four of the Owen family members were enjoying the laughter and joking atmosphere. The move to a new house, the changes that came with starting a new job, the "tightening of the belt" to make ends meet, seemed to actually make this a happier family than before. The tension they all lived under had dissolved into feeling of being a family. John continued his sessions with Mrs. Jane, the kids were doing well in school and Jan didn't mind doing without now that her family life was calmer and much happier.

"So what about you guys going up there? I think it's your turn now." This time no one was laughing at John's statement.

"Really? You think we should go up there too?" Toni and Russel said the same thing at the same time, which made everyone start laughing again.

"Sure, but only if you really want to. It can't be something you don't feel really drawn to do."

"You know, we could probably go to the pastor and talk to him about it first. You know, to help us make that decision. That might help to understand what it means." Jan said. This helped the kids feel they didn't need to do it just because their Dad had done it.

"Once again, my dear, you have a great idea!" John made a dramatic bow to his wife to which she held out her pretend dress and made a very lady-like curtsey.

All this playfulness got the kids to start giggling again.

The next day at the supper table, Jan announced that she had called the church. She told her family about how they could meet with the pastor a few times if they'd like and talk about what it meant to ask Jesus into their lives. To this, everyone seemed to be in agreement.

"I like this idea WAY better than Dad's idea of just going up to the front." Toni spouted out. "That idea kinda had me a little freaked out."

"Gee, I couldn't tell, Toni." Her Dad said with a bit of sarcasm to his voice. "I mean, your eyes nearly popped right out of your head when I mentioned going up there before."

"Yeah Toni. You looked like you were about to jump right out of your chair when Dad said that!" Russel joined his Dad in giving his sister a hard time.

"If I remember right, you both about fell over when I mentioned it. Even your Mother's eyes popped a bit when I laid that bomb on you guys!"

"I gotta admit, it did take me a bit by surprise!" Jan confessed. "But I think it'll be great for our family to work on our spirituality. And Toni, they do have a Sunday school program. When they mentioned some of the families that go to that church, I recognized several of them from your class."

"Awesome! I'll miss Mrs. Mason though. She's really sweet. Maybe someday, if Jill stops being such a jerk, she can come to Sunday school with me!" Toni, always hopeful, brought a smile to her Mom's face.

"How come you're picking me up?" Jill was surprised to see her sister pull up to the school instead of her mother.

"Mom, Dad and Levi are meeting with the lawyer so I'm taking us out to get some supper." Olivia said in a very matter-of-fact tone.

"Hurry up and get in! I'm starved!" Bobby hollered.

As the car pulled up to the Chicken Shack, Jill seemed a bit put out. This was usually the place they'd go when Toni was with them. Jill was starting to think of the good times she and Toni had shared. She was beginning to miss her friend. Her *real* friend. The three ordered their food, sat in the dining area and barely said a word to each other. It was obvious they each were having a hard time processing what was happening with their family. Not talking about it was probably the worst thing they could do, yet that's what they did.

"You gonna finish that?" Bobby pointed to Jill's almost untouched chicken.

"No, you can have it." quietly, Jill replied.

"Is there something wrong with it?" Olivia asked.

"It just doesn't taste right." For some reason, Jill just didn't like the taste of the chicken this time. Something was missing.

But if serving the Lord seems undesirable to you, then choose for yourselves this day whom you will serve...But as for me and my house, we will serve the Lord.

Joshua 24:15 NIV

CHAPTER FIFTEEN

WHAT GOES AROUND, COMES AROUND

It was a very tense time at the Turnbaugh household. Levi was arrested for selling pot. There was no amount of talking Mr. Turnbaugh could do to get him out of it this time. This was a very serious offense. When word got out around town about the arrest the baseball league Levi coached, relieved him of his duties. An article with Levi's picture was published in the local paper. This, of course, got the whole town talking. Levi was looking at spending some jail time and maybe even some prison time since he was 18 years old. Even with only a couple of weeks before graduation, Levi wasn't going to be able to graduate with his class. Jill, of course, was totally mortified. How was she going to face the kids at school? She begged her Mother to let her stay home for the rest of the year. But there was no way Mrs. Turnbaugh could let her do that.

Jill wailed, "But the other kids know what happened! What will they think of me?"

Mother, brushing Jill's dramatic argument off, told Jill, "I'm sure they'll be fine. Kids your age rarely understand about things like this anyways."

Well, Mother was wrong. The kids noticed. They knew very well what had happened and looked at Jill like she had some horrible, contagious disease.

As Jill was coming around a corner in the hallway, she heard some kids talking.

"I can't believe he was arrested!"

"I know! He must be a real druggie."

"Well now everybody knows what kind of people they really are."

"Yeah, they may seem all fancy and upper class but they're just plain old white trash. That's what my mom said anyways."

"I don't want anything to do with people like that."

"Me either."

Jill was frozen in her steps. She wanted to go around the corner and tell them what she thought about their cruel words but just then the bell rang. At the end of the school day, Jill saw Brittany, Kelsey and Heather. She was sure they'd stick up for her.

"I know this is going to hurt, Jill. But we just don't think we can be friends anymore." Brittany started.

"But what my brother did, has nothing to do with me. I didn't do anything wrong." Jill was trying to hold back the tears.

Kelsey added, "Well still. Maybe you should just go hang out with Toni."

Heather continued, "Even though you didn't have any sympathy for Toni when her family got in trouble maybe you two have more in common than you think. Plus my mom said I needed to stay clear of you and your family."

In unison, Brittany and Kelsey replied, "Yeah, so did mine."

With that the three girls turned and walked away. This was Jill's worst nightmare coming true. All Jill ever wanted was to be popular and have friends. These were the friends she thought cared about her and now they had turned their backs of her when she really needed them. By this time the tears were rolling down Jill's face. She headed for the restroom, went into a stall and sobbed uncontrollably.

As Toni was waiting for the bus after school, their new friend, Alan walked up beside her to wait for the same bus. Alan and his family recently moved to Morely. His father worked at the same farm as Toni's father. A few times a year, the farm would put on a large supper for all the employees and their families. The last get together was held a week ago. Toni, Russel and Alan met there and became quick friends. The three started making plans to make a go-cart out of a bunch of scraps they found in various locations around the farm. Alan and his father, Bill, did a lot of projects like this. They both had a knack for carpentry and mechanic work.

"Hey Toni! Where's Russel?" Alan surprised Toni, who was deep in thought.

"Oh, you scared me!" Toni said as she jumped a little.

"Sorry. I didn't mean to scare you."

For only being a year older than Toni, Alan showed a great deal of maturity and manners.

"That's ok." Toni smiled. "I'm not sure why Russel's not here yet. He'd better hurry or he's going to miss the bus. It's a long walk home!" The two chuckled.

Just then Russel came running up behind them. Out of breath, Russel greeted his sister and new friend.

"Phew! I'm glad I didn't miss the bus! I was talking to Bobby. Did you hear about Levi?"

"Yeah. It's all over school. You'd think no one had anything better to do than gossip about other people's problems." Toni said with disapproval. "How's Bobby doing? I didn't see Jill all day. I'm kinda worried about her. This is the kind of thing that'll really freak her out."

"Bobby's alright. He's disappointed with Levi. But he's hoping this will be the kind of thing that'll get Levi to pull his head out of his butt." Russel replied. "As for Jill, maybe she's getting what's coming to her for being such a jerk to you."

Alan, trying not to eaves drop on the conversation between the two siblings, watched as the bus pulled up.

"Hey, Alan! Are we still on tonight for working on that go-cart?" Russel turned to Alan with excitement in his voice.

"Sure thing!" Alan was glad for the awkwardness to be over. "I've just got a couple of chores to do and then I'll ride the 4-wheeler over."

"Perfect. We've got some chores to do too and then we'll be ready." Russel and Alan continued to talk about the details of the project as they got on the bus.

Toni sat quietly on the way home. Her mind was drawn to Jill. Even though the two hadn't spoken in a long time, Toni still cared about Jill and couldn't help but feel bad for her. She knew first-hand how tough this kind of family problem can be. Toni thought back to how just a few months ago, things had been so different for both families. At such a young age she was still able to grasp what a twist of fate both families had taken.

Silently, Toni began to pray. *'God, thank you for helping my family to be happy again. Please help Jill's family to be happy again, real soon. Amen.'*

"Do not judge, or you too will be judged. For in the same way you judge others, you will be judged, and with the measure you use, it will be measured to you."

Matthew 7:1-2 NIV

CHAPTER SIXTEEN

CONFESSION IS GOOD FOR THE SOUL

"What are you doing out here without a fishing pole?" Bobby was confused to see his little sister at the fishing pond. Jill was just sitting on the shore, no fishing pole, no friends, just by herself. The look on her face showed the heartache that was consuming her.

"I just needed some time to think." Jill was very somber. Bobby saw a hint of tears that had been rolling down her face.

They hadn't been getting along very well lately. Bobby had been upset with Jill for the way she had been treating Toni. Whenever he brought the subject up, Jill became very defensive, didn't want to talk about it and usually stormed off.

Showing concern for his sister, he asked, "What are you thinking about?"

"I'm thinking about how much I miss Toni." Jill's voice quivered. "I wish she was here right now and we were trying to out-fish you and Russel."

"Have you talked to her lately?"

"No. I've been too busy trying to make friends with a bunch of selfish snobs."

Bobby chuckled. "I noticed."

"I know you think I'm a real butt-head for the way I've been treating Toni." Jill was getting upset now. "You tried to tell me, but I was a real butt-head to you too." Now the tears were starting to flow again. "I just want things to go back to the way they were. Nothing makes sense and I'm scared for Levi. Is he going to have to go away? Mom and Dad won't say anything about it around me. I've asked and they just say it'll be alright. When are we going to be able to see him again? "

Bobby was trying hard not to show Jill that the tears were welling up in his eyes too. He moved closer to Jill. "I'm sure we'll be able to see Levi soon. I heard Mom and Dad talking that he may have to spend some time in jail, but they didn't think it'd be that long."

"You know, I thought what Toni's family was going through was such a big deal. I acted like it was the end of the world! Now our family is going through this! This is way worse! Not that what Toni's family was going through wasn't bad."

"Toni and Russel's family seem to be a lot happier now. The only thing keeping us from being happy is how we deal with it all. Toni's family took what happened and dealt with it. They didn't try to hide it or make a huge deal about it. Bad things happen sometimes. We just need to accept it and make the best of things."

For being a young man, Bobby was showing great maturity in helping his sister deal with her fears.

Bobby continued, "Toni's family is happy because they dealt with the problem and chose to be happy. We can do the same thing. It's going to be hard knowing that Levi is in jail, but we can talk to him, write to him and maybe even visit him."

"The girls in school act like I've got some horrible disease and they need to stay clear of me." Jill stated with a little more conviction in her voice.

"Those girls are shallow and self-centered." Bobby said, matter of factly. "All they care about is how things look and how things affect them, not about other people's feelings. Real friends don't care about things like that. They look at who we are and care about us no matter what."

"Toni told me that she forgave me for treating her the way I did. I was so rude to her. Do you think she'll ever want to be friends again?" Jill began to cry again.

"If I know Toni like I think I do, she'd love to be friends with you again. Toni and Russel are real friends. Not fake ones that only care about themselves."

"Maybe Olivia can drive me over to their house so I can talk to Toni. Will you go with me?"

Bobby looked at his fishing pole and then over to his sister who was finally acting like her old self. Rolling his eyes, he knew he couldn't say no to her now. "I suppose. Besides, I want to see this go-cart that Russel and the new kid are building."

The two headed back to the house and found their older sister. Jill told Olivia what she wanted to do and asked her to drive them out to the Owens house.

"You know, little sister, I'm proud of you for realizing how important Toni is to you. As much as I like to hang with the popular kids, not all of them are nice people. Sometimes you need to see them for what some of them really are...snobs. Most of them have never experienced anything hard or uncomfortable in their lives. They've never been taught how to be tolerant or understanding to others. So when something bad happens, they don't know how to show others sympathy. " Olivia put her arm around her sister's shoulder. "So I'm glad you finally woke up and realized you're not like that. But before I take you over there, go wash all those tears off your face and comb your hair." Olivia may have been understanding but she still wanted her little sister to look presentable.

"Russel, the phone's for you. It's Bobby." Mother called out the door.

"I'll be right back." Russel told Alan. "Maybe Bobby will come over and help us with the go-cart."

"We can use all the help we can get." Alan joked.

"Hey Bobby! What's up?"

"I was just wondering if you were home. Actually, Jill was wondering if Toni was home. She wants to come by and talk to her. She's just being a big cry baby and made me call."

"Really! Wow! Yeah, we're all here. Am I supposed to tell Toni she's coming?

"I don't know. Jill's finally pulled her head out of her butt and wants to apologize to Toni."

"That's great! I'm sure Toni will be happy to talk to her. Alan's here too. We're working on the go-cart. You want to help us?"

"That'd be great! I've been wanting to see it!"

"It's coming along pretty good. Alan's really good at this kind of stuff. I've learned a bunch!"

"K. See ya in a bit!"

"K. Bye!"

"Is that the Turnbaugh's car?" Toni asked her Mom as she watched the car come up the drive.

"Sure is. Bobby called Russel a little while ago. They must be going to work on the go-cart together." Mom replied.

"Olivia's driving and I think I see Jill in there too." Toni was a bit confused and curious.

Looking out the window, Mom agreed that Jill was in the car along with Olivia and Bobby. "Maybe she wants to talk to you."

"I don't know. She hasn't said anything to me for a long time."

"Well, you won't know until you go out there and ask her." Mom encouraged Toni.

"What if she just wants to say more mean things to me?" Toni was feeling very apprehensive.

"I can't imagine she would come all the way out here just to be mean. Would you like me to go out there with you?"

"Yeah, maybe she'll be nice if you're there."

As the car came to a stop, Bobby jumped out and joined Russel and Alan in the shed. Olivia got out from behind the driver's seat. "Hi Miss Jan. Your new house is so pretty!"

"Thank you Olivia. Would you like to see the inside?"

"I'd love to!" As Olivia walked into the house with Jan, she turned to see Jill slowly getting out of the car.

Toni stood just outside of the house. The suspense was driving her crazy. Should she stay there and wait for Jill or should she go in the house with her Mom and Olivia.

Just then Jill spoke. "Hi Toni."

"Hi."

"I like your new house. It's really pretty."

"Thanks."

"Toni, I have something to say to you."

Toni was wishing her Mother was there by her side. She didn't know what to think or what to say. The last time she and Jill spoke, well, it wasn't pretty.

"Ok."

"Toni, I've been a real butt head lately. I've treated you like crap and I'm really sorry." Jill let out a big sigh. "Can we be friends again? I really miss you."

Toni stood there, frozen. She was so surprised at what Jill just said that she couldn't believe it was real. This was something Toni had been praying for. And now her prayers were being answered.

"I'd really like it if we could be friends again. I've really missed you too."

With that Jill ran up to Toni and hugged her tight. "Thank you for forgiving me."

On their way home Olivia couldn't help but to tell her little sister how proud she was of her. "You know, Jill, I'm really proud of you for seeing who your real friends are. Hanging with the popular kids is all well and fine but you need to realize that just because they are popular in school or their family has money doesn't give them the right to be rude and hateful. Being tolerant of others shows class. It was really good to see you and Toni back together again."

"Thanks Olivia. Hanging with those other girls was hard work. I felt like no matter what I did, it was never good enough. It feels good to be around Toni. She lets me be me."

"I'm really glad you apologized to Toni too. Now maybe we can have some fun again!" this was Bobby's way of telling Jill he was proud of her too.

Confess and acknowledge how you have offended one another and then pray for one another to be instantly healed, for tremendous power is released through the passionate, heartfelt prayer of a godly believer!

James 5:16 TPT

CHAPTER SEVENTEEN

REPENTANCE OPENS THE DOOR TO HEALING

It was the time of year for the Morely Annual Go-Cart Race that was held at the high school track. The three boys were busy making last minute adjustments, talking over strategy and trying to look cool in front of all the cute girls that had come out for the go-cart race.

VOICE THROUGH THE LOUD SPEAKERS: "Welcome to the Morely Annual Go-Cart Race! This year we have several new entries, which makes the races all the more exciting! We'd like to thank all the participants, volunteers and sponsors that have blessed us with the largest donation in the history of the races.

If you're not familiar with the Morely Annual Go-Cart Race, this is our 6th annual race. All proceeds go to help fund the Morely Animal Shelter. As always we'll start out with the Bantam category. Would all the participants line up at the starting line please? The Bantam category is for the 6 and 7 year olds. They will race from the starting line to the beginning of the curve on the track. While they're getting set up I'll continue to explain the rest of the races. The next category is the PeeWee category. This is the 8 and 9 year olds. They'll race from the starting line to the second curve of the track. Next is the Jr. Category. This is the 10 to 12 year olds. They will race all the way around the track. Then our oldest group, the Senior category, which is the 13 and 14 year olds who will make 2 laps around the track."

"I think having to wait so long for our category is going to drive me crazy!" Alan said with so much excitement that Russel and Bobby busted out laughing. It wasn't like Alan to be so nervous.

"I know! Maybe we should go get something to eat from the concession stand." Bobby said, trying to get their minds off the wait.

"We need someone to stay by our cart so no one messes with it." Russel added.

Just then Jan and John Owen walked up with hotdogs and sodas. Toni and Jill were with them, carrying bags of chips.

"Would Team Olsen like a little snack since you have to wait awhile yet?" Jan said as she handed out the food to the boys.

Team Olsen was the name they decided on since the Olsen Ranch sponsored them and gave them most of the materials to build their go-cart.

"We knew you wouldn't want to leave your cart unattended so we brought the food to you." John added in.

"Thanks!" all three boys shouted in unison.

"This is the first time we've ever been in the pit! This is way better than sitting in the stands!" Toni could hardly contain her excitement.

"I can't believe how many people are here! I think this is the biggest turn out the race has ever had!" Jill was getting caught up in the excitement as well.

As the boys were finishing up their hotdogs and were sipping their sodas, they saw two go-carts being pushed up by four older boys. So far they felt pretty confident about the race. The only other contestants in their category was a team the same age as them. Plus the other boys were a bit on the awkward side. Since Bobby, Russel and Alan were athletic and strong for their age, they felt they had the advantage over the other contestants. But now the older boys showed up and whatever confidence Team Olsen had was quickly melting away.

"I really wish I hadn't eaten that hotdog now. I think I might throw up." Alan couldn't stop staring at the older boys as they pushed their go-carts up closer.

"Don't worry about them Alan. You boys are just as capable as they are." John said to comfort the nervous boys.

"How many do they have on their team?" Russel was trying to assess the situation.

The boys kept a close eye on their opponents. Two more boys showed up. The two teams had matching t-shirts. Each team had 3 members just like Team Olsen. It seemed like forever for the other categories to finish but the time had finally come. The Senior category was up next. Since this race went around the school track twice, they were allowed to switch off drivers. Each team was allowed three members and that's just what each team had.

Russel was going to be the first driver, then Bobby with Alan bringing up the rear. It was time for them to push their cart to the starting line. The other drivers took their positions on the track where they would take their turn at driving the cart. By this time Team Olsen had a large following of Jan and John, Alans parents, Fran and Nash and even Mr. and Mrs. Olsen. The boys could hear them cheering them on. They also could here Jill and Toni cheering.

"Go Team Olsen! Keep up the pace! Go Team Olsen! Win this race!"

Even though the cheer was a bit corny, it lightened the mood and the boys were starting to enjoy themselves. The voice over the loud speaker boomed: "Alright now it's time for the Senior category. In this category we have Team O'Brian, Team Carter, Team Olsen and Team Wilson. Is everyone ready?" Each team gave the thumbs up.

"On your mark, get set, GO!"

Russel took off. He peddled the go-cart as fast as he ever had. He was neck and neck with Team O'Brian, one of the older boy's cart. Next was Team Carter and then Team Wilson, the other of the older boys' cart. As they approached the 2/3 mark where they would switch off drivers, Russel was at a slight lead.

As Russel brought the cart to a stop, Bobby jumped in. Russel gave him a good push and away he went. The slight lead that Russel made seemed to be getting bigger. As Bobby rounded a corner he noticed Team Carter's cart cutting in on the inside track. How could this be? There was no way he was going to let the smaller, less athletic team get ahead of him. So Bobby gave it all he had. Team Carter didn't have what it took to keep the lead and soon Bobby was in the lead again.

Alan was jumping and cheering as Bobby pulled up to change drivers for the last leg of the race. Team Olsen had a good lead but then Bobby recognized the last driver for Team Wilson. Brian Wilson was a track star in school. He hoped Alan could stay ahead of him. Alan took off like a rocket. Team O'Brian was gaining on Alan. Team Wilson and Team Carter were neck and neck.

It was the last curve of the track. Team Olsen was losing the lead they had to Team Wilson. Alan could see them out of the corner of his eye. The last 50 yards to the finish line Alan poured it on! He could see his team mates jumping up and down just past the finish line. Team Wilson was gaining on him but Alan didn't let up.

The checkered flag waved in front of him but he wasn't sure who had actually won the race. He knew Team Wilson was right there next to him. Then he heard the voice on the loud speaker.

"Congratulations Team Olsen for a split second win!"

'Holy Moly! We did it! We won!' the thought went through his mind and then he heard his team mates yelling the same thing!

Russel and Bobby ran up to the go-cart and helped Alan bring it to a stop. The three boys were jumping up and down with excitement. Soon they were joined by their parents, family and friends. The other racers came up to them and congratulated them as well. The driver of Team Wilson came over and shook Alan's hand.

"That was some amazing speed you had going. Have you ever thought about going out for track? We could use someone like you on our team."

Being the new kid in school, this made Alan feel really good. "Thanks. I'll give that some thought."

After all the awards were presented and the crowd started to thin out the three families put the go-cart on the trailer.

"How about I treat everyone to a celebratory supper?" Nash Turnbaugh announced.

"Chicken Shack!" everyone yelled.

"Chicken Shack it is!" Nash agreed. "How about we all meet over there?"

Another round of "Sounds good." came from everyone.

As Toni and Jill were catching up to the others who were heading to the parking lot, Jill saw David Jacobs. They hadn't spoken much since the incident with Levi. David's Dad, Officer Jacobs, was the officer that brought Levi into the police station.

"Hey David!" Jill called out.

"Oh hi." David responded.

"That was a great race, wasn't it?" Jill continued.

"Yeah. Hey I gotta tell ya something. I don't think we can hang out together anymore. You know with that thing with Levi and all. My Dad was pretty upset that Levi lied to him about the pot."

"Oh, ok." was all Jill could think to say.

David turned and walked away. Jill went over to where Toni was waiting for her.

"Well I guess David and I broke up." Jill explained to Toni.

"Oh no. I'm sorry Jill." Toni said sympathetically.

"You know I don't feel mad or sad or anything like that. I feel kinda sorry for David that he can't see me for who I am. I'm not just the sister of someone who got busted." Jill confessed.

"That's called forgiveness Jill! I think you finally get it!" Toni was excited for her friend.

"Yeah! I think I do forgive him for thinking the way he does! Jill was a bit shocked even at herself. "I feel so much better not holding a grudge about it! Let's go have some chicken!"

"Sounds good to me!"

And off the two went to catch up with their families.

At the Chicken Shack, they ordered enough chicken strips, side dishes and even desert for everyone. The parents sat at one table, the kids at another. Everyone was enjoying the spoils of a great victory and wonderful fellowship with old and new friends.

"The chicken strips sure taste a lot better than the last time we were here." Jill stated with a hint of confusion as to why they tasted so different.

Olivia leaned over to her sister and whispered. "Maybe it's not the chicken strips that are different but the person eating them. The last time we were here you had a very different attitude."

Jill stopped for a moment and thought. Her sister was right. The last time she was here, she was missing her friend. At the time she thought there was something wrong with the chicken, but what was really wrong was her attitude. Jill looked to her friend sitting next to her and smiled. It was so great to be friends with Toni again.

"Well Toni, I guess we'll have to get busy and make our own go-cart for next year." Jill said very matter of fact. "We can't let those boys out do us."

"Absolutely! I've been thinking the same thing. We could be Team Cool Chics." Toni replied without a hesitation.

From the parents table you could hear a resounding "Oh good grief!"

Be kind and compassionate to one another, forgiving each other, just as God forgave you.

Ephesians 4:32 NIV

CHAPTER EIGHTEEN

NO SKUNKS ALLOWED

"This place is great!" Alan told the Fab Four as they showed him the fishing pond.

"The fishing's pretty good too!" Russel explained.

"We've caught the biggest fish here and if it weren't for that stupid skunk we would have had the most too!" Jill boasted.

"A skunk?" Alan said while he wrinkled his nose.

"It chased us up a tree and took the fish we had on the stringer." Bobby continued.

"We should show him the tree! We want to build a tree fort in it. It's huge!" Toni led the way to the tree.

As they approached the big tree the Fab Four had taken refuge in, they all stopped and stared at it in awe.

"Wow! That sure is one big tree. It really would make a great place for a fort." Alan said almost mesmerized.

"Let's go back to the house, get a tape measure and paper. Then we can come back out here and start making plans." Bobby announced.

So the now Fab Five did just that. Once they got the measurements of the tree they headed back again to the house to draw up a rough sketch of the fort they wanted.

"What are you five up to?" Olivia's curiosity was showing.

"We are making plans for our tree fort." Bobby said, very business-like.

"What tree do you plan on building this in? The trees in our yard sure aren't big enough. Plus, I'm sure Mom and Dad wouldn't let you build it where everyone could see it." Olivia retorted.

"What won't Mom and Dad let you build?" Mr. Turnbaugh said as he came in the room.

"They want to build a tree fort." Olivia said with an air of tattling.

"A tree fort! Gosh, that'd be a hoot!" Nash got excited about the idea.

"Father, you can't be serious! You're going to let them build a fort in one of our trees in the yard. That would look so trashy!" Olivia objected.

"We're not going to build it in the yard, so there!" Jill defended.

"Dad, there's a really big tree out by the pond that would make a great tree for a fort." Bobby appealed to his father.

"Really! I guess it's been a long time since I've been out there." Nash continued to sound interested.

Just then, Fran Turnbaugh walked through the door.

"Hi all! Well it looks like an important meeting is going on here. What's up?"

"Hi Mom!" Jill jumped up and gave her mother a hug. "We're telling Dad about the tree fort we want to build."

"Oh my. I don't think any of the trees in our yard are big enough to support a fort. Plus that would really bring the value of the house down." Fran, being a realtor was thinking in terms of her business.

"The kids said there's a big tree by the pond that they want to use." Nash added, defending the kids.

"Oh, will that be safe for them to be out there like that?" Fran switched gears from business owner to mother now.

"Mom, we're not babies." Bobby protested.

"Yeah Mom, we're not babies." Jill got her protest in as well.

Olivia just rolled her eyes and left the room.

"Well I guess it's safe to say that you won't have to worry about Olivia crowding you out of your fort!" Nash joked.

"So we can build it?" Bobby shouted.

"Well, let's go out and take a look at this tree first." Nash added before he gave his final approval.

The five kids and Nash all headed out the door. Fran stated she was going to change her clothes and start supper. After supper, and a great deal of discussion about the tree fort, Mrs. Owen came by to take her kids and Alan home.

"Mom, Mr. Nash said it's ok for us to build a tree fort in this big tree out by the fishing pond!" Toni blurted out as soon as the kids got in the car.

"Well, that sounds exciting."

"Mr. Nash started telling us about the materials we need and how to build it so it's safe." Russel added.

"Yeah, we were just going to use some scrap wood that's behind that old barn at the ranch." Alan added.

The kids continued to talk about the materials, how they were going to do the work themselves and how much fun they would have in their fort. As they pulled in the drive, the kids saw Mr. Owen and Bill standing by one of the out buildings.

"Dad, Dad!" Russel barely waited for the car to come to a full stop before he jumped out and ran to his father. Alan and Toni were right behind him.

"Hey kids! What's all the excitement about?" John greeted his very excited children.

"We're going to build a tree fort at the Turnbaugh's pond."

"The tree is huge!" Alan added.

"Mr. Nash gave us some great ideas." Toni informed the men.

The three kids were all talking at once. Finally John got the kids to calm down enough so they could get the full story about the tree fort.

"This is quite the ambitious project you kids are taking on." Bill admitted. "How about we set down and draw up a plan and figure out what materials you're going to need.

"That's a really good idea." agreed John. "How about after supper tonight?"

"Sure. I can do that." Bill agreed. John and Bill continued to talk as they walked away.

The three kids stood there, a little shocked, a little confused. While it was great to have the approval of their parents, they felt a bit left out of the process.

"What just happened?" Russel looked at the other two.

"They're kind of taking over our project I think." Alan replied

"Do you think they'll do it without us?" Toni asked.

"Nah, they wouldn't do that, would they?" Alan had a very confused look on his face.

The three didn't really know what to think.

After supper Alan and Bill arrived at the Owens house to draw up the plans for the tree fort.

"I called Nash and he wants us to come over to look at the tree and draw up the plans." John told Bill as they came in the house.

"Wonderful. We can take my truck." Bill agreed.

John and Bill headed out the door. The three kids jumped up and followed them out. They were still getting the feeling of being left out.

At the Turnbaugh house the three men went out to look over the tree. Again the kids jumped up and followed.

The three men took measurements, then headed back to the house with the five kids in tow. Once at the house the men sat around the table and begin to draw up plans for the fort.

As Olivia walked passed the table, she looked at the plans. "You should really put a window on the east side as well as the west side so you'll get good lighting. They could even hang some plants in the east window."

The Fab Five simultaneously rolled their eyes.

Fran happened to come in the room as Olivia was giving her opinion and agreed with her daughter. "That's a great idea, Olivia. What about a picnic table and chairs on the ground. It would be like having another room." The realtor was coming out of Fran again.

More eye rolling came from the Fab Five. Having everyone but themselves decide what to have for the fort was starting to bother them.

Leaning over to the others, Alan whispered, "I've got an idea. Let's go outside and talk." The five got up and went outside. The others in the house didn't even noticed they were gone.

Once outside and a good distance from the house the Fab Five went into conversation that lasted until the others came outside when it was time to go home.

"Well, I think we've got this project figured out." Bill announced.

"Yup. We can't work on it for a few weeks but we'll get it done." John added.

The kids just smiled and got in the truck.

School was out for the summer, so the Fab Five had a lot of time to put their plan into motion. No one noticed their coming and going out to the pond, nor what they took with them.

A week later they invited their families out to the pond. It wasn't easy getting everyone to come out at the same time but they managed to pull it off. As the adults approached the pond and looked over to the tree. Their mouths dropped open in surprise.

There was a wonderful tree fort! It had four walls, a floor and a roof. There was a window on each side and a ladder leading into the floor entrance.

"Holy Moly! Look at that!" John hollered out.

"Wow, that's impressive!" Nash added.

"That looks great kids!" Bill proudly agreed.

"You kids did this all by yourselves?" Fran asked.

"Yup!" The five said in unison.

"Can we go in it?" Jan asked.

"Sure! We'll give you the tour!" Jill offered.

The adults were so amazed at the amount of room there was once inside the fort. The men examined the carpentry work to make sure it was safe. To their surprise, it passed with flying colors.

"You kids did an amazing job." Bill again said with pride.

___

After the adults left, the Fab Five sat in their tree fort. The feeling of pride they shared was evident by the smiles on their faces.

"Well, we pulled it off." Bobby announced.

"Yeah, I wasn't sure we were going to get the lumber here from the ranch without anyone noticing." Russel added.

"I don't think we could have done it without Mr. Olsen. I'm glad he kept our secret and hauled the lumber for us." Alan admitted.

"I have a little surprise for everyone." Toni announced. She went to her backpack and pulled out a piece of wood. On the front of it she had painted, "NO SKUNKS ALLOWED!" Then she hung it on a nail on the wall.

They all laughed and agreed that was a good sign to have. As they sat in their fort, talking, joking and laughing, they all stopped at the same time.

"Oh no! What's that smell?" Jill asked with a horrifying look on her face.

"SKUNK!

THE END

To some who were confident of their own righteousness and looked down on everybody else, Jesus told this parable:

"Two men went up to the temple to pray, one a Pharisee and the other a tax collector. The Pharisee stood up and prayed about himself: 'God, I thank you that I am not like other men – robbers, evildoers, adulterers – or even like this tax collector. I fast twice a week and give a tenth of all it get.'

But the tax collector stood at a distance. He would not even look up to heaven, but beat his breast and said, 'God, have mercy on me, a sinner.'

I tell you that this man, rather than the other, went home justified before God. For everyone who exalts himself will be humbled, and he who humbles himself will be exalted."

Luke 18:9-14 NIV

Made in the USA
Monee, IL
26 July 2020